A TO Z OF ORIGINAL POEMS, FLASH FICTION AND SHORT STORIES

ANDRÉE ROBY

© 2020 Andrée Roby

Cover Illustrations: Elysia Paine & Micaela Grove

Editing: Régine Demuynck

Publisher: Régine Demuynck

ISBN: 9798634833101

Ce livre est dédié à ma mère, Monique Demuynck.

CONTENTS

PREFACE

The idea of an A to Z of stories came from attending a Creative Writing Club. Members had to write a one page story based on a word or sentence. I used my stories and various people suggested words for letters I was missing. I am very grateful to everybody who contributed a title. As a writer, it has been a fascinating journey to come up with over twenty stories on totally different themes.

Heartfelt thanks to my daughter Micaela and my friend Sue for their willingness to read my words at various stages, to encourage me and challenge me.

This book was finished during the lockdown of 2020 caused by the Coronavirus. I trust the lessons learnt at the time will be remembered in the future. I am grateful for the dedication and commitment all of the key workers who kept the country going and to everyone who helped others in this difficult time.

My sincere thanks to Mark, Anna, Lois, Julienne, Dee and Micaela who looked out for me during my self-isolation and made sure I had enough food (and chocolate).

Andrée Roby – April 2020

"Don't come in here Sophia. Go back outside and get the neighbours to call the police."

Steve was shouting at me, pinned down on the kitchen table by my father who was holding a knife to him. With amazing strength he managed to grab the knife and broke it in two with his bare hands. He pushed my dad away from him. Dad looked at me, pushed past me and ran outside.

"Don't come in here Sophia. Stay out."

Steve was warning me again but I had to see my mum. I had heard a dreadful scream from outside the house and I knew it was my mum. I had heard that scream on many occasions so I needed to check how she was. Had my dad hurt my mum again?

I rushed into the kitchen, disregarding Steve's warning. My mother was lying in a pool of blood.

"Dad stabbed mum."

That terrifying, cold statement came from somewhere in the recess of my young mind. I was only ten years old. My little sister, standing a few metres behind me in the hall, was eight.

"Go to the neighbours Annie, tell them to call an ambulance, hurry."

I was suddenly in charge of getting some help although it was obvious my mother was dead, stabbed several times. Steve, my mum's new boyfriend, had nearly been killed too. And my dad had done a runner...

How can I forget the sight of my mother that day? Or the traumatic, hard-to-believe reality that my own father had killed her. This time he had gone too far and stabbed her to death. I knew they argued a lot and he often hit her. Never did I imagine that he might end up killing her.

At that moment I hated him. I hated him because I loved him and he had hurt me and my sister. I hated him because suddenly mum was no longer around. He had deprived us of our mother. That day my dad had become a monster in my young eyes.

I had always known my dad had been obsessed with my mum to the point of wanting to control her. Even during their many periods of living apart, he still wanted to dictate her life. They had broken up so many times in the ten years since I had been born. From a young age life at home had been difficult and stormy. I had realised that my dad didn't treat my mum well but I also knew mum loved him to death – literally, as it turned out. They were two people struggling to live together yet couldn't bear being apart. What security and stability does a child of such a couple get in life? Dad was not a dad, he was my father. Their relationship was more off than on. Life at home when dad drank too much was unbearable. So during the off-periods, Annie and I were happier.

Before the day of the murder, the worst day of my life had been when my mother had asked my dad to come back to live with us. That was only nine months before he killed her. I told her no. I had an inkling things might turn out bad. She didn't listen. Mum needed a man by her side at all times, and right now dad was the man she wanted. She was addicted to him despite the physical and mental abuse. I struggled with him being at home. Within a few months, mum threw him out again after dad put her in the hospital for three days. Will she ever learn? We moved away. We had some time away from him, making a happier life for the three of us. Mum had got a new boyfriend, Steve, who was nice to her and to us. He was good for her and for a while I was happy. But it didn't last.

Dad had heard that mum had a boyfriend. That sent him over the edge. He had lost control of her. So that fateful day, he had come by the house on the pretence of taking Annie and me out to the park. First he had sent us to the shops to get some drinks and sweets for the outing. We were gone less than ten minutes. He used that time to attack mum, stab her and then try to kill Steve who had come home shortly after dad's arrival.

I was glad that he was arrested quickly and jailed. But life after the murder was unstable and harsh. Annie and I went to live with our maternal grandparents in Ireland. I was still reeling from the shock of it all. Apart from that one kiss on my mum's cold forehead the day before the funeral, the realisation that we will never, ever, see or kiss our mother again was heart-breaking. To top it all, a few days after the funeral I was expected to go to school as normal.

Everyone acted as if nothing had happened. But plenty had happened. Nobody talked about my mother or about my father anymore. He was in jail, she was buried, and life went on. I rebelled. I needed to talk about mum. I needed to understand why dad had killed her. Part of me wanted to talk to him and ask him why? How is a child to comprehend the enormity of such an act? How can a child come to terms with one parent being murdered and the other parent being their killer? I needed support, professional help, reassurance and love but got none of those. I was unable to cope. I lost my temper easily at school. I blacked out and had more and more angry outbursts. That scared me. I thought I was exactly like my father. I feared my temper was bad and that I, too, might be a killer one day. No-one explained to me this was normal and all part of the grieving process in such tragic circumstances.

My dad was convicted of my mum's murder six months later. It was a relief that he had been given life imprisonment, with a minimum of ten years to serve. I worried that he might come out of jail and this time come after me and my sister.

Life was bad for me, living at mum's parents became stressful. I yearned for them to love Annie and me, and help us through this ordeal. It took me years to realise they were grieving and they didn't know how to support us. I had started to run away. I had suffered such severe trauma but no-one was there for me. I went off the rails and my grandparents were no longer able to cope with me. I was sent to live with my mum's sister and my five cousins.

Life then took a different turn. My auntie expressed her view that maybe I ought to write to my father and get his side of the story. Maybe he had acted in anger and had not intended to kill my mother after all. I had to think hard about this. Part of me wanted to hear some soothing words, proving to me that my dad was not an evil monster. That maybe he had loved her instead of just wanted to control and abuse her. That he was sorry for what he did to her and to Annie and me.

The letter I finally received said none of those things. Instead it firmly put the blame on my mother. He claimed that he had got angry because she told him I didn't want to go on any outing with him and that my sister was not his child. I was vulnerable, I needed someone to lean on, something to grab onto as I was sinking further and further into a nightmare abyss. I established a relationship with him. Many years later it dawned on me I had been manipulated into believing that it was not his fault, that my mother had goaded him. At the time, I chose to believe he was not completely to blame. That my mother had a share of responsibility in her own death. I gained some temporary relief from this false way of thinking because despite everything, I still loved my dad. After all, he was all I had left in this world. I had no idea that my father was a psychopath. He was a heavy drinker who became aggressive and violent under the influence of spirits. His short fuse lead my mother to end up in hospital several times.

Then dad was released from prison. How that had been possible I do not know to this day. He had committed murder and served only eleven years. The minute I agreed to renew a father-daughter relationship with him, something in me snapped and I started drinking heavily. The rest of my family was no longer talking to me because of my bad behaviour and my drinking. I was ostracised. I had no-one to turn to except my dad, the killer. My uneasiness around him and my drinking were nothing compared to the events that unfolded a couple of months later.

Dad told me he had met a woman, Danielle, who was the same age mum had been when he killed her; twenty nine years old. Similar sense of style and character. Alarm bells rang in my head. I met Danielle on a few occasions and found her lovely. My dad was controlling towards me now and towards his new girlfriend. Once I told her to get out, that dad had killed my mother. Sadly he had convinced Danielle that it had been an accident and she had believed him. Eventually though, his true colours showed and Danielle ended her relationship with him.

I kept telling my dad not to enter into a relationship as he was released on licence but he ignored me. I was worried but I didn't do anything. My dad was not supposed to enter in a relationship, drink or do anything illegal but no-one checked on him. His parole officer knew nothing about what he was up to. I regret I never rang him to alert him to dad's new relationship. A few months later, dad killed Danielle in a similar fashion he had killed my mother. My anguish at losing my mother was compounded by my guilt at not having taken steps to prevent Danielle's murder. This lack of action on my part haunts me as much as the sight of my mother's body.

Life has not been kind to me. I was robbed of a mother, of the innocence of childhood. I have been manipulated by my father, I have been ostracised by my family. And all as a result of my father's decision to kill my mother. Luckily, despite everything, I found someone who loves me and who is helping me cope with all the traumas I have suffered. Often, when a murder is committed people think of the poor victim. Only few have any inkling of the impact of the murder on other members of the killer's family. This was my case….

(Based on a murder which took place in the UK in the late 90s.)

THE BUTTERFLY WITHIN (POEM)

In the first part of my life,
I was a caterpillar and a wife.
I enjoyed my caterpillar life!
But, in truth, problems were rife.

I made my way to my cocoon
Like caterpillars do, but much too soon.
I thought it would last till doom
But maybe I was hoping for the moon.

The cocoon was nice and snug.
Life was decidedly smug.
Till one fateful day full of pain,
To bits my world was slain.

Through life I ploughed on,
To my cocoon hanging on,

Very slowly misery moved on.
After all, the transformation had to go on.

The caterpillar was no longer a wife.
The butterfly had to start its life.
Wings and antennas started to emerge
As gradually with independent life I merge.

Every day my cocoon opens a bit
Even if time passes before I leave it.
Of my new life it is the beginning
For now, I am a butterfly with purple wings…

"What the caterpillar thinks is the end of the world,
the butterfly knows is only the beginning."

July 2000

C
THE COPPER KETTLE

Will they, won't they? They have sniffed around me for ages.

I looked at the woman who was holding me, inspecting me this way and that, for the last few minutes.

"It is so beautiful. Look at it, Albert."

"It's a bit old fashioned," the man said dismissing his wife's enthusiasm.

"Albert, you don't understand anything. Of course it's old fashioned, that's the vintage look. The copper body and the whistling sound when the water boils are so quaint. Let's get it please… It's only £5."

£5? £5? My goodness, I knew stuff sold cheaply at car boot sales but £5? For me? A bona-fide whistling copper kettle? It is an insult.

I was outraged, offended, disgusted and upset all

at once. Who would have thought how low my life had got. I will have you know that, when I left the workshop of the kettle maker, all shiny and new, it was 1929. Yes, 1929. I have lived and survived a war and many, many decades.

My first ever family had been the Jenkins. Oh how I loved them. Mum Jenkins was careful with me. She kept me shiny and clean so I whistled happily every day when the strong fire on the stove brought the water to the boil. I remember her looking at herself in my shiny belly. She was pretty, Mum Jenkins. Him, I didn't care for too much. He was a bit rough to be honest. Every time he filled me up with water, he banged the lid down. What a brute. Did he not realise how unpleasant it was for me?

Then they had three Jenkins babies. My proudest moments were on the days those babies were born and I boiled the water needed to clean them up. Oh it was so wonderful to be part of the family and of the children's lives. How many times I gave them hot water to clean their grazed knees, to warm their feet in winter, and to give them warm tea when they were cold. So many happy years.

Alas, it came a time when the Jenkins babies left home. They were all grown-up. Mum Jenkins gave me to the middle child, Joe and his wife Dorothy. They had no money so Mum Jenkins wanted to help them out when they moved into a rented flat after their wedding. She parted with her beloved copper kettle. And do you know something? She cried when she let me go. I saw her with my own whistling spout, I cried too that day. Mum Jenkins was sort of a mum to me too.

So, there I went, to Joe and Doty's place. (Doty is how Joe called her by the way.) I was often dirty during my years there. My whistling was not a happy one anymore. My bottom hurt from them banging me unceremoniously on the stove. It was a strange stove, that one. Not at all like the one Mum Jenkins had used. I thought I was going to pass out at Joe and Doty's house. I think they consumed more hot drinks than food, so I was always on the go. I felt exhausted and often wondered what had Mum Jenkins got me into. I reassured myself that she can't have known what her slob of a son was like, or she wouldn't have given me to him. I had to believe this or I would stop whistling altogether out of sheer sadness.

One day things turned even stranger. I found myself on this tall, slim plastic table in a place all stark, with white walls, which I heard people call "a museum". I just sat there, all day, being examined from all angles by museum visitors. I was "Exhibit 10 - Copper kettle from early 20th Century". Many times a day I heard people reading the white little card in front of me so I knew what it said by heart. I felt useless. I was no longer whistling. I was redundant, almost at the end of my life. Was I really going to spend the rest of my days in a museum?

"How did I even end up there in the first place?" I hear you ask.

Well, it was Doty's fault. She wanted to appear to go up in the world and had convinced Joe to buy her an electric kettle. I was shocked. A kettle, without a nice round belly, hooked by a lead to a place in the wall and which does not even whistle? It was so ugly, its body transparent, showing the water boiling inside. Indecent if you ask me. Even stranger, there was a blue light shining from the bottom of this modern contraption whilst the water boils. So not fetching. I observed it from a distance as I was relegated to a corner of the kitchen worktop. No longer in use, no longer in favour.

What was my fate going to be now? Well I didn't have long to wait. She sold me to a Museum of Antiques for £15. The years I was there were the worst of my life. Yes even worse than at Joe and Doty's place. At least, at theirs, I had a purpose. Now I just sat on that pedestal, bored and useless. I was polished a couple of times a week by this guy who thought nothing better than to blow his fetid breath on my belly and then rub it with a dirty cloth. I wished I was able to twist my spout away from his horrible breath.

Miraculously, my ordeal ended one day when the exhibition was dismantled. I was snapped up by a museum employee who wanted to make a bit of money. He took me to the car boot sale. So there I was waiting once again to see what will become of me.

If only I had known at this junction in my life what awaited me. Jane, Albert's wife bought me for £5. Despite my initial outrage at the miserly price tag, this turned out to be the start of a love story I am still living to this day. Jane loved me, she looked at me often and lovingly stroked my body with a soft cloth. I occasionally whistled when she put me on a gas cooker but, on the whole, I was a display in a modern, wood and glass cabinet.

Again, I hear you ask yourself:

"Why is this kettle happy to be on display after its time at the museum?"

Well, let me tell you. It's because a miracle happened. In that cabinet, I met the most beautifully engraved, daintiest copper kettle from a faraway land which she told me was called "Tunisia". Her name was Leila and I was in love… Leila described the exotic land, she was born in. It was a land full of sand, storm, colours and sun. She had been sold as a souvenir at a local souk ("a local market", she explained). Jane and Albert had brought her back to their own country ("the UK", I informed her).

I sat next to her, on a glass shelf, our spouts touching. Occasionally we were both taken out of the cabinet to be admired by some of Jane's friends or dinner guests. Jane proudly showed us off. Until I came along, Leila had been sitting pretty but lonely on that shelf.

Now there we were, happy, in love, and so proud to be cherished displays in Jane's house.

D

THE DOG SHRINK

Will this epidemic ever end?

I wondered wearily after my fifth appointment of the day. I was exhausted already and I still had to see another six patients.

What on earth did I get myself into?

It was not the first time I asked myself this question. I had retrained about two years ago and I thought it was the right way forward at the time. I had studied for four years for my previous job so I might as well build on that and diversify. I liked the idea of being a counsellor and the rewards were not bad either. But I never imagined how busy I was going to be.

This is relentless, so many patients needing my attention. Phew! Busy times indeed and no sign of easing off. More and more dogs seem to have emotional issues. What a world we live in.

"Nurse, please call the next patient in."

I looked up as the door opened. I saw a well-dressed woman, mid-forties I thought, ushering her pooch in to see me. She almost had to propel him forward as the poor mutt was decidedly scared of entering my office. It was a fairly stocky Labrador, clearly lacking in self-confidence and extremely stressed. It was unusual, so I wondered what had brought this on. Being such a sociable breed, the dog should be gregariously walking in, seeking some kind of contact with me. What had made him so scared and reluctant to come and see me?

"Hi. I am Melanie. This is Roddy. He is having panic attacks. He is a quivering wreck when I leave the house to go to work. When I come back home, there is a mess everywhere. I am at my wits end with him. He is scared of everything and I don't know what to do for him. Can you help please?"

Oh Christ! There we go again. Another dog who is having panic attacks and who is depressed and misbehaving. This is serious. That's the 15th dog so far this week who has emotional issues. And it's only Wednesday, what's going on with these patients?

"Hi Roddy. Hi Melanie. Tell me more about the behaviour that the panic attacks cause? Does he jump at people, bark, chew furniture, toys or things? Is weeing and pooing inside part of the problem as well as being all excited when you get home?"

18

"Yes all of that. I leave at eight in the morning to go to work. He has toys to play with, so it's ok isn't? When I get home around six, I give him his dinner and let him out for a toilet break in the garden. I know I should walk him every night but by then I am so tired after the whole day at work…."

No wonder then, is it? Poor dog cooped up all day and no walks. Excuses, excuses, woman… God, I am so sick of such ignorance. It is now up to me to remedy the emotional damage caused by the owner. Worst still they don't even get that if you don't give suitable living conditions and exercise for the dog, misbehaviour is the likely outcome… Well, that's another one to treat, right here, right now.

"When I do walk him, and it's raining, I put his lovely coat on. It's a Burberry coat for dogs. Would you believe it, though? He barks, refuses to go out or rolls on his back in the street to try and take it off. I buy the best raw meat. It is expensive but I feel Roddy doesn't appreciate all that I do for him. He is lucky to have all I give him really. And he is famous too, who wouldn't want that. I take pictures of him at week-ends and he has 1,000 followers on Instagram. Seriously I don't understand this dog. He has a great life and he does not appreciate it…"

"Yes I understand the problem better now. I am glad you brought Roddy to me today. He certainly needs to be a normal dog. Don't worry I can help turn things around. Roddy, sit. Good boy. Now wait and settle Roddy. Good boy."

"Ok. Melanie please lie on the couch, and let's get this treatment started. Roddy will be better in no time at all. Now repeat after me: I shall walk my dog twice a day, even when I'm tired. I will be patient with him and not leave him alone all day long without someone walking him at least once a day.

I shall not, under any circumstances, dress him up, make him pose for pictures and plaster said pictures on Facebook or Instagram. I will respect that he is a dog and not a toy or an exhibit. I shall be grateful of his delirious welcome when I get home. I shall not focus on the pee, or other mess, left on the floor out of boredom and desperation because it is my own fault. Have you got that Melanie? Good girl.

Ok, Roddy off you go, take your mum home and make sure she treats you well from now on. Good boy."

Well what did she expect? I may have retrained as a shrink but I am still a vet at heart. I have never seen so many dogs recently with so called mental issues though. Loads of them depressed, lonely and misbehaving. Am so glad I did this counselling course. At least now I can treat the owners in good faith and they can't argue with me. But seeing their faces every time I ask a patient to jump on the couch. What a picture, what a laugh. That is a classic. As if the dog needed a shrink? That's how little they know.

Mind you, it does say "Dog Shrink" on my door. But it doesn't say who I treat. That makes me laugh every time. Oh I love my job.

E
EATEN ALIVE

It's a day like any other in the sub-Saharan African savannah. A day when I spend most of my time high up in a tree, resting under the cool shade of sumptuous foliage, like a small umbrella, shading me from the harsh African sun. I love resting on the branches of high trees. I'm unique in this way. Not many of my fellow felines can climb the way I do. I'm amazing when I'm in action. You should see me. I am agile and so strong that I'm able to carry warthogs and antelopes up my tree. I don't want these giggling hyenas or prancing lions to get my prey, do I? So I climb far up. You would not believe how powerful my claws are. I keep them sharp too. When I walk, I hide the claws in my paws so as to not blunt them. Clever isn't it?

When I want a change or when I 'm tired, I seek out a big rock and lie in its cool shade but still I prefer hanging from a branch in a tree. Today I fancy a swim. Yes, a swim. That's what I said. Why? You don't know I swim? I'm a strong swimmer and I'm hoping to catch a few fish and find some crabs too. I deserve such delicacies from time to time.

I bet you can't guess what my favourite part of the day is? Apart from feeding time of course. Well, it is coming soon. The day is ending and the most stunning sight is revealed. I see it every day and I'm still in awe of the African sunset in my savannah. It is just like the horizon catches fire and the land, the rocks and the trees get painted red and orange. And then as the sun finally goes down, the curtains open and I see the star-filled African sky. I like to contemplate the awesomeness of it. Plus I know that once the sun goes down, it is my time to go and hunt to feed myself. I may be a killer but I can still admire the beauty of my habitat.

Slowly my whiskers direct me towards a prey. I sense it when I'm near. I hear the prey breathe. I'm silent and powerful. I climb the nearest tree. What I love best is to pounce down onto my prey right underneath the tree. Some of the antelopes are so dumb, they don't realise I can jump on them. I favour that. I can't be bothered to waste all my energy in high-speed chases like lions or tigers indulge in. I believe in preserving my energy and I'm doing well. I have survived for six years so far.

I'm lucky no lions or hyenas have ever managed to get me.

Actually it nearly wasn't the case. My mother told me that I was almost eaten alive by a lion when I was a cub. She had gone to get some food and left me with my brothers and sisters hidden in vegetation but this old lion fancied a snack. Luckily he didn't see me as I was camouflaged by my spots, but he got my little brother. Mum called him a Panther, he was all black. Why he was called differently than us I don't know? The fact is the poor cub stood out so the lion got him instead of me. It saddened me to lose Panther but I'm happy to be alive and to enjoy my life in the savannah.

Recently, on my journeys, I came upon some strange looking creatures standing on their two hind legs. They walk around in packs and make strange noises. They travel in the savannah in a metal box on wheels which smells bad. I know that such creatures live a short distance from my favourite spot. As I didn't recognise their breed, I didn't fancy chasing them or eating them. I left them well alone.

Tonight on my way back to my tree, I come face to face with two of these creatures walking towards me, holding strange sticks they point out at me. A clapping noise erupts and an orange fire suddenly comes out of the sticks. A bright orange fire like the orange sky of my savannah. I feel a sharp pain going through my leg. Another clap and the pain explodes in my rump. Then one final clap heralds a sharp pain in my heart. Life is slipping away from me. I had survived being eaten alive as a cub and had hoped for a long life. The Universe (or humans to be precise) had decided otherwise. For tonight the neighbouring tribe is rejoicing at eating leopard meat. Then, in a few weeks, my yellow spotted pelt will adorn the floor of one of their huts. Deep inside my soul, I wonder if I will ever again see a stunning African sunset.

F
FEEL FREE

"Passengers for flight EZY8691 to Las Palmas please make your way to gate sixty nine. The flight is ready to board."

In my chest my heart is thumping with excitement. It is incredible that people around me don't hear the noise it is making.

"This is my flight. I'm going to Gran Canaria."

I fill up with exhilaration as I make my way to gate sixty nine. I have finally managed it. It took me six months of savings to afford a break in Las Palmas. This is my treat for my fiftieth birthday and I will be celebrating it in Spain.

I still have difficulty realising I am at Gatwick Airport, on my own, ready to board a flight to a destination I have never been to. If it was not for the documentary I saw on the special beaches and the sand dunes in Las Palmas, I would never have thought of going there. Not mentioning the unusual night clubs with the flamboyant characters that perform there every night of the tourist season.

I feel positively like Shirley Valentine. I was twenty years old when I saw that film in the late eighties. I had just got together with Chris, who was thirty two, so I didn't understand why Shirley wanted to go on holiday on her own, leaving her husband behind. But after twenty years with Chris, I know why she needed to do that. Like her, I want to experience freedom while I am still young enough to enjoy it and wise enough to make the most of it. I want to find out who I am and what I am capable of outside of my relationship with Chris. Because this trip is a game changer. This is an experience my heart has hankered for practically all my life but didn't have the courage to go for.

Well, in a few hours, I will land in Las Palmas, get a taxi to the hotel, have dinner and spend my first night abroad. Then in the glorious, sunny morning I will make my way to one of the most stunning, secluded, sandy beaches in Las Palmas. My heart flies out of my chest, I am that excited.

I feel a twinge of guilt as I left a note for Chris on the kitchen table to say I am taking a break. Purposely, I didn't mention anything beforehand about my impending trip and my absence from home for my birthday. Again I blame Shirley Valentine for my devious plan. Mind you, I am pretty sure that apathetic Chris has not organised anything special for me anyway. So I am glad I have taken charge of my own celebrations.

Suddenly, I stop in my tracks. People walking to the boarding gate behind me, bump into me and tut loudly. The enormity of what I am doing suddenly hits me. What on earth possessed me to consider this unusual adventure? I know that to feel free I have to experience who I am. This includes giving in to my inner desires. I guess I still feel I will be judged as weird so I keep quiet.

I love Chris but I need some excitement in my life. The age gap means that we are at different stages in our life. Mine had been stale and I felt stuck in a rut for quite some time. Then, out of the blue, the magic of Gran Canaria became an irresistible pull. I am in for a treat and I want to make the most of it. The only unknown in my mind is whether I will go back home to what I know or stay on and live a totally different life.

My experience of the nude beach tomorrow is the first leg of my adventure. To feel the sun, the sea, and the sand on my naked body is tempting. To meet like-minded people on the secluded beach is even more exciting. I would never dare to do that back home so I am super happy.

Then, of course in a few days, after getting a bit of

a tan, I will be executing the second part of my plan, the icing on the cake. I had worked hard at convincing the manager of the transvestite nightclub to let me perform as Miss Valentine. Of course he had no idea if I was any good but he relented, allowing me to perform for one night only, the night of my birthday.

I had brought my favourite dress, accessories and make-up to dazzle him. I had practised with a dance teacher for nearly a year so I now danced like a pro.

This is my dream come true, dancing on stage to celebrate my fiftieth birthday. The thought of Chris at home, sitting in his chair, watching EastEnders, makes me want to stay here. I am still a young man with plenty of life inside me.

So watch out Las Palmas, Miss Valentine is coming.

G
GO AND GET IT!

As a child, she had always been competitive at school, in her studies and, unusually for a girl in the nineteenth century, she excelled in sports. In her twenties, she chose a career as a travel writer. Not the sort of occupation a lady chose to have but there was something in her that made her different than her peers. She may have been born a girl but this was not a limitation in her eyes. She had thrived to excel, ensuring that she became the best in her field. For this purpose, she had learnt several languages and developed her knowledge of world geography. Being the best travel writer was no mean feat for any gender in the late nineteenth century.

Travelling anywhere took a long time as the steam trains were slow. Horse-drawn carriages took days to reach any destination and were often unreliable. Boats were cumbersome and extremely slow too.

Cars had only just appeared and were beyond the reach of most people. However, with resourcefulness and determination, she had managed to travel to, and write about, the United Kingdom and most of the European countries.

In 1895, she had even gone to America and reported on New York, on the immigrants who had settled there from various European countries. She was asked by an English newspaper to write about Ellis Island where most of the immigrants started their new life in the States. Her collection of articles on various aspects of the life in America had added to her credentials as a female travel writer and generated a handsome income. But she was not satisfied with this, she wanted more.

What had helped her stay at the top of her game so far had been her love for travelling and foreign culture and, of course, being competitive. She also had a strong pioneering spirit. Her great ambition was to discover and write about a country or a place that no-one else had ever written about. Not easy when the majority of the planet was being explored by mankind. She began to check atlases and read other travel writers' books to identify any potential area which had not been widely covered. She yearned to get that special scoop, the acknowledgement that she was the best. And the only way to achieve her goal was to go and get it for herself. Get the glory and recognition for finding an untapped treasure. Despite her research and ambition, she drew a blank until one day when fate dealt her a winning card.

It was late 1905, and during a brief visit to France, she met a French speleologist. She had never before known anyone who studied caves for a living. Being open-minded and still in search of "the scoop", she let herself be convinced by the speleologist to travel south to Provence and to the Alps. She wasn't sure if this would turn out to be a waste of time, but something told her to trust her new friend Édouard Martel and to accompany him on his project.

Édouard had been commissioned to survey a twenty five kilometre gorge in the Alps, in order to tame the river Var and use it to irrigate nearby fields. The aim was also to provide drinking water to two major towns; Toulon and Marseilles. Exploring what is now considered as Europe's Grand Canyon, Édouard found a treasure which no one, beyond people in Provence, were aware of. It was a deep expanse of water of the most stunning turquoise colour, running over twenty five kilometres, with rocks on each side and waters nearly one kilometre deep. France owned a jewel called the Verdon Gorge which the country had not even been aware of. This was the scoop she had been waiting for.

Who better than her to inform the rest of Europe

of this stunning unspoilt beauty spot. In 1906, she finally wrote about the discovery in a magazine published in France, which triggered tourists to come and discover the area. At last she had achieved her goal. She had given tourists somewhere to go that had been unknown and that, in her eyes, made her the best travel writer in Europe.

Now in her eighties, she still remembered the feeling of success, exhilaration and sheer jubilation at the publication of her article all those years ago. She remembered the lesson that she had learnt then; no-one will hand anything to you in life, so if you want something, go and get it yourself. She had lived by this for a further three decades and had done well for herself. She blessed the day she had decided to follow her instincts and had gone with a man called Édouard.

H

THE HALLUCINATING HEAD TEACHER IN HARROW-ON-THE-HILL

This is a humorous story I will hasten to tell.

This story hails from the day the Head Teacher of a primary school in Harrow-on-the-Hill, Henry Harriott, decided to harness any budding musical talent in his school. Our local hero, as he saw himself, went on a hunt for musical instruments that would hurtle the children towards their illustrious musical careers. He hunted down harmonicas, cellos, guitars, flutes, recorders. He even heralded a new era in the school by acquiring a harp. No-one had ever heard of any of the schools in Harrow-on-the-Hill owning a harp. This will be a feather in the Head Teacher's cap and he will position the harp in the assembly hall, on the side of the stage, in full view of every one.

Who knew what talent would hatch from his handiwork? Henry had always harboured the dream of discovering a highly musical child and turn the poor mite into a hyped-up success. He had hardly been a musical prodigy as a child. On the other hand, his parents had been humble people but world-renowned pianists. Clearly, in his case, talent was not hereditary. Hence, he was all in favour of helping the children find their own path and achieve their potential. However, the Head Teacher had decided that only the year-two class was to be given a chance to be harbingers for the school new musical venture.

Happily, a week later, the instruments were delivered to the music room. The delivery company was on a hectic schedule so the instruments had been left in a helter-skelter manner, laid out everywhere and in no particular order. At the sight of such goodies, all the children went hyper. To prevent the whole class from wreaking havoc, those who had shown a healthy interest in playing an instrument were invited to point to their chosen device. Then they calmly had to wait for it to be handed out by the music teacher, Hugo Hurley.

With hindsight, it was farfetched to expect a six year old to find the right instrument for him/her. But honestly, the children seemed to find the right one for each of them and the music teacher was impressed.

Hugo, at times, was a bit harsh and high handed but he was willing to work on this heart-warming project to form a homogenous group of budding musicians. He knew the Head Teacher held the vision that the children hooked by the music, would get into the habit of practising some harmonious tunes and hymns. He thought his boss' vision was a bit too high-flying for the school. Imagine trying to find a talent amongst this bunch of have-nots from the poorest area of Harrow-on-the Hill. Not being the one at the helm though meant he had to follow orders.

"Right then, let's see what happens next. Let's hear them play." The Head Teacher said.

As soon as he gave the go-ahead, the children started playing, any which way, creating a huge cacophony. The teachers and the other children witnessing this display were in hysterics. Never had they heard anything so hickledy pickeldy.

"My Goodness" thought Henry "this horrible sound hurts my ears. Please let there be some harmony."

Suddenly, he heard a most harmonious sound coming from the assembly hall, half-way down the corridor from the music room. Was he having some sort of hallucination? Was his hearing playing tricks?

He hurried towards the sound and halted as he saw a child playing a haunting tune on the harp. Habitually he didn't pay much heed to this half-pint child. He identified him as Olli, a boy from a poor home. He did wonder how on earth such a half-wit was able to play so well. He was not being hard-hearted or hurtful about the boy, it was merely that he had been told by the teachers that Olli was hard-pressed to do simple work correctly in class. How to explain his talent then? Talk about a hidden gem. Listening to him now, the Head Teacher had a hunch this kid would go far with the right help. He felt hell-bent suddenly on hiring a private teacher for Olli, someone he would hand-pick to ensure that nothing hampered this boy's progress.

He approached Olli and praised his performance. Olli looked up at the Head Teacher, remaining silent.

"Olli. Well done, that was wonderful, I want you to play the haunting tune you just played at tomorrow's assembly. I am not sure where you learned to play like that but it is such a heart-felt rendition. I want to hear it again. Is that alright with you Olli?"

The child nodded hastily albeit silently. At the start of the assembly the following day, Olli was sitting by the harp. The Head Teacher introduced him:

"Children, silence please. I have asked Olli to be the highlight of our assembly today. He is going to play a tune I heard him perform yesterday. Frankly I wasn't aware we had such high-class talent in year-two. Please clap to welcome Olli."

The children excitedly did as they were told. Olli shrugged hopelessly towards his peers and pulled on the strings. The sound that came out was nothing short of horrid. The Head Teacher was horror-stricken and unable to comprehend why Olli's rendition was so horrendous. The harp was groaning under the heavy-handed assault on its strings.

"Olli stop, stop right now. Why are you not playing what you played yesterday? Stop horsing around will you."

"But Sir I am playing the same tune. I can't play to save my life. Yesterday was the first time I touched a harp. Sir, honestly, I can't play."

The Head Teacher sensed the hair on his back rise in panic. It had all gone haywire. He hastily left the hall to the sound of children huddled together laughing at him like hyenas. He was so humiliated. What had happened? Had yesterday's performance been an hallucination after all?

I

INCREDIBLE COINCIDENCE OR HEAVENLY INTERVENTION?

I shall let you, the reader, come to your own conclusion. But first, let me recount a true story which I found so touching I wanted to share it in my book.

This is how it begins.

Katie, a single mum, decides to get a kitten as a companion for her young daughter Holly. They go to their local animal rescue centre and see these two gorgeous, white and ginger kittens, both male and born of the same litter.

They look like identical twins. Their little faces so innocent - as only a kitten's face can look - and all fluffy. They are only twelve weeks old. Both mother and daughter fall in love with the two brothers but unfortunately they have to choose one. They have moved to a new flat in a big city and the landlord has a one-pet only policy.

"I know it is a hard choice, Holly, but we need to choose one. Which one though?"

After much dithering and a mixture of excitement and sadness, they settle on one of the kittens and take him home. They decide to call him Ozzy.

But Ozzy finds it hard to settle and is sad, clearly missing his twin. A few days later, Katie rings the shelter to find out if the other twin is still there, just in case. Her plan is to approach the landlord about allowing them to have both cats. But the second kitten was adopted four days after Ozzy.

Holly is upset. Katie reassures her: "don't worry, I have a feeling that maybe one day the brothers will see each other again."

Ozzy settles finally and life goes on.

Katie, fed up with being single, signs up with an online dating agency and meets Barry.

"I'm lucky, he is such a nice man."

The sort of man she has been wanting to meet and to settle with. She is glad to have Holly but yearns to have a normal family too.

It turns out that Barry has lost his wife, Sue, and has a young daughter, Jess. She is the same age as Holly, ten years old. Katie and Barry go on a few dates, get to know each other and really enjoy each other's company.

One evening, Katie is invited to dinner at Barry's house. On arrival, she does a double take. She sees

Ozzy wandering around this house although it's not his home. She is baffled. She and Holly do not live far from Barrie but far enough for Ozzy not to have wandered into Barry's house. Of course she knows some cats are prone to visiting homes other than theirs but not Ozzy. She wonders if he has stolen her cat, but how, when and why? She questions him, feeling a bit unsettled and annoyed at this unexpected turn of events. Barry is just as taken aback when she accuses him of stealing her cat. He is adamant Butter is his cat and he explains to Katie how he joined their household.

Life was sad for Jess whilst her mum was ill and certainly since she passed away a year ago. Before passing, her mum had given her a wonderful present to remember her by. She wanted so much to bring the young girl some happiness in her time of sorrow and grief. Sue had got Jess a gorgeous, white and ginger, boy kitten from the animal rescue centre. They had christened him Butter. He had lived with Barrie and Jess for a year now. Much like Ozzy, he was a well-loved, well-cared for companion. Katie resolves to take Barry back to her place in the morning and introduce him to Ozzy.

"If he is still there", she can't help thinking. Of course, she believed Barry's story is genuine but she is still somewhat baffled.

The following day when they arrived at Katie's

house, Ozzy is there to greet them and it is Barry's turn to be surprised.

"This is my cat".

Katie shakes her head in denial. "No, it isn't but I know what this is about."

She brings out the adoption paper for Ozzy. She asks Barry when and where he adopted Butter. Barry recognises the date of birth which is the same as the date his own kitten was born on. He also confirms that he got Butter from the same rescue centre as Katie adopted Ozzy from.

"Mystery solved then. What a fantastic reunion. The twins are reunited after just over a year apart. Brilliant. Wait until we tell the girls, they won't believe it."

"That's for sure. What an incredible coincidence. You know what, I think my departed wife had a hand in us meeting, through these kittens. Wouldn't you say?"

"Yes, this definitely looks like a case of heavenly intervention. The brothers are reunited, our daughters are sisters and we have each other. It's what I've always wanted, a whole family. I'm so happy. Thank you Sue and thank you kittens."

J
THE JUDGE

The envelope on the door mat looked so ordinary that it was hard to imagine this little paper wrapper was capable of changing the Judge's life to the extent that it did in 2015.

To understand what that envelope represented, one had to be aware of what the Judge's life had been about. Then of what had happened to him as a result of falling in love, for the first time, at the ripe old age of sixty five.

The Judge had been a respectable judge upholding the law for the last thirty five years. He was a well-known pillar of the justice system in London's Crown Courts. Everyone who came in contact with the Judge was struck by his affable demeanour but also by his appearance: his height, the way he carried his body so tall, his spine erect. When he donned his wig, he seemed even more powerful and scary to the numerous offenders who appeared in his court room for sentencing.

The Judge had such an air of authority and quiet self-confidence that even the most belligerent offender didn't dare argue with him. His sentencing was fair and he usually only passed sentence after extensive consideration of the case in hand. His position as a judge had been his life since being a young man and he had not had the time, or the inclination, to get married. His career meant way too much for him to allow himself to be distracted by relationships or worse - in his learned opinion of course - by marriage. He assumed that if he was involved emotionally and romantically with a woman, he might lose himself and jeopardise his career. Strange thought really. Millions of people are perfectly capable of holding a demanding job and have relationships. Not the Judge though. He had resisted getting involved with anyone for years. That is why, at sixty five, he had never been in love, lived with anyone or been married. He paid regular visits to accommodating ladies - as he described them - but only ever spent an hour or so in the chosen lady's company and only every couple of months.

That was until early 2010 when Jane showed up in his court room. Jane Edith Davies. He remembered how her name had sounded like honey to his ears. It still did five years later. This slip of a woman had appeared in front of him for murder. It was the most unusual murder case he had presided over. Jane Davies had stabbed to death the poor guy she had been married to for five years, had been arrested and charged with murder. She had admitted to the murder but had refused to this day to explain her motive. The police officers had probed and probed but she had not uttered a word of explanation as to why she had killed the man she was married to.

The Crown Prosecution Service had also failed to secure a motive for the murder. The two defence barristers struggled to put together a reasonable defence case to present to the jurors, based on the little information available to them. The evidence at the scene of the crime contradicted a possible self-defence theory. The probing into the couple's relationship had not turned up anything alarming which might have provided an explanation. A psychologist had been brought in to speak to Jane about her reasons for keeping silent but that had produced no result either. Everyone who had been interviewed was shocked at the turn of events as the couple were perceived as being close and in love.

It was a total mystery. This case had greatly piqued the Judge's curiosity. This was his first murder case without a clear motive. So far anyway. The accused had not denied the murder, or attempted to plead for a reduced charge of manslaughter. However she expressed genuine remorse for having committed such a terrible act. All of this made little sense to the Judge.

Since the beginning of the trial, the Judge's mind had been in overdrive, figuring out a motive. He had created an elaborate tale of deceit, mental and physical abuse carried out against Jane by her husband. All in all the invented story was making him feel mellow towards the accused.

As the trial started to unfold, the Judge became aware of some stirrings in his heart, body and, more embarrassingly, in his groin every time he saw Jane sitting in the dock. She was only five foot four, slim, with shoulder length blond hair and a round angelic face. The settings were not glamorous or conducive to romance for sure, but there was something in this woman that made him hot under the collar. It was so out of character for the Judge that he struggled with it until he finally admitted to himself that he fancied her. She was cute to look at and serene too. It was that which made him desire her. Her serenity! The Judge had conveniently skimmed over the fact that she was in the dock, accused of murder. Was this not something to be concerned about instead of lusting after an alleged murderess?

He most certainly ought to have stepped down there and then but, for the first time in his thirty five year career as a Crown Court Judge, he refused to do the right thing. He planned to stay on and see the trial through to the end.

The trial was progressing well. The defence team had brought in various character witnesses who appeared in front of the judge to attest of Jane's good standing. Experts had been sworn in to give their opinion on her possible mental state as she refused to talk about her reasons. On the other side, the CPS's experts explained in gruesome details how the victim was murdered and brought different experts to explain how her silence regarding her motive was a sign of an evil, manipulative and deranged mind. With each new expert, the jurors seemed more and more baffled and unsure as to who to believe.

On the first day of the second week of the trial, the accused, via the barristers, had asked to speak to the judge in his chambers to divulge privately, and only to him, the reason for her crime. This was unheard of but in view of the lenient disposition the Judge felt towards the accused, he granted her an audience. They were in his chamber for half an hour with a guard standing by. The judge didn't appraise the jury of what had transpired but sent the jurors to deliberate on whether they considered Jane to be guilty of murder or not. They had been informed by the judge to agree unanimously on a verdict. The fact that Jane had pleaded guilty of murder and not of man-slaughter meant that her sentence had to be life imprisonment and it was up to the Judge to decide the minimum sentence she had to serve before an early release was granted.

Upon its return, the jury had decided on a verdict of guilty. Their decision had not been an easy one as the jurors felt that the lack of a motive didn't give them full knowledge of what had happened. On the basis of what he had heard from Jane, the Judge sentenced her to life as required. But he took the most unusual and most controversial step of sentencing her to serve only a minimum of five years instead of the statutory minimum of fifteen years. The CPS was in shock and protested. Even the defence team was not sure what was happening. The only ones who understood were the Judge and Jane who exchanged a long meaningful look before she was taken away to a prison cell. The Judge left the Court feeling skittish and dizzy all at once. He had done something unheard of, him, the pillar of respectability. But it had been worth it. In a few years Jane would be out of jail. She had promised him something wonderful: he needed to be patient for the next few years to get his reward.

In July 2015, the Judge was found lying on the floor by his front door, having suffered a heart attack. In his hand, he was still holding an envelope and a card. The card read: "There is no fool like an old fool... Yours gratefully, Jane."

K
A KNOCK ON THE DOOR

In an old-fashioned house, throning on top of a green hill in Cumbria lived a rather strange-looking young woman.

"Strange" might be a bit strong. Maybe unusual would suit her better. Her hair was long, blond and often not brushed. Her fashion sense was non-existent. She favoured flowing Indian skirts which were more 1978 than 2018. Sandals adorned her bare feet whatever the weather, prompting the question of whether she had a stash of similar sandals as they never varied in style only in colour. Her tops were also seventies style and she wore oversized jumpers on cold days. Definitely not the usual appearance of a Cumbrian resident.

Villagers at the bottom of the hill were intrigued by her but only a few of them actually knew anything about her. Some said her name was

"Emma" and others swore that they heard her call herself "Laura".

One thing they all knew is that she lived alone in the house which used to belong to a distant cousin of the Royal Family, namely on the Prince of Wales' side. The cousin had died but some villagers still remembered him. She had come to live in the village a few months ago. There were rumours that she was mid-twenties but her hippy-looking style didn't do her justice. Often she looked like a weirdly dressed thirty something.

There were speculation as to how she was able to afford to buy the big house at the top of the hill. She was never seen going to work, and only glimpsed doing her shopping in the village once a month. The rest of the time she roamed the countryside in search of herbs, plants, flowers and bushes or stayed indoors. When villagers came across her, in woods or fields, her arms were always laden with various greenery picked that day.

Tongues wagged constantly: "She must be a witch", "Maybe she is a herbalist", "This is strange, her not working and roaming the hills".

On and on it went…

Emma or Laura was aware of the interest she generated but ignored it most of the time. She got on with her business, an activity which made her extremely happy. About once a fortnight a white average-size van with no markings, would drive steadily up the hill to the house. Then, as observed by nosy villagers, the driver would park at the back of the house, go in for about half an hour, then load boxes in the van and drive back down the hill to join the main road leaving the village.

The curiosity down in the village was rampant. Many craved to have a peek at what was being loaded in the back of the van? These comings and goings were too mysterious and unnerving. People needed to know, didn't they? In case the girl was up to something dubious.

One day, the worse gossiper in the village, Ethel, decided to enlist the help of a few cronies. To ensure their participation in her crusade, she whipped up a frenzy of assumptions about the weird one, as she was known in the village. Assumptions not only outlandish but mainly negative and derogatory.

So it was that one March morning, when the van was due to go to the house, Ethel and her posse of three ageing gossipers like herself, braved the walk to go to the house on top of the hill. It took them a little while but they got there as the van was still parked at the back.

Ethel asked: "Who is going to knock on the door?"

Secretly she thought she was entitled to be the

one to knock but she also wanted to appear magnanimous so she had raised the question.

Gertie replied: "You, of course, Ethel, I think you should be the one to do the honours. It was your idea after all to come here."

No sooner had Gertie finished her sentence that Ethel approached the front door and knocked with a firm, decisive thump on the beautiful wooden carved door. Nothing happened at first. No-one showed up to answer Ethel's demanding knock. She was none too happy.

"I say, I'm sure she is in, but she is not answering. How rude of her."

As Ethel ranted to her friends, the front door suddenly opened and there stood the weird one, dressed in her usual seventies attire, her blond hair today held in a messy bun overflowing from every part. Up close, the women saw that she was most probably late twenties.

Ethel was taken aback and stuttered her "hello" then carried on;

"My friends and I wanted to introduce ourselves and see if we can be of help to you. I am Ethel by the way…"

This statement was clearly designed to elicit a reciprocal introduction but the weird one, standing in the doorway, just looked at her, saying nothing.

Ethel's curiosity was aroused so she went on:

"I don't know your name but we are so pleased you chose to come and live in our village. We wanted to introduce ourselves, this is Gertie, Barbara and Iris. As I said, we wondered if there was anything we might assist you with to settle in?"

"Hello ladies. Thank you for taking the trouble to come up here and for your kind offer but I am fine. Now I am afraid that I need to return to my work, I have to photograph my spring creation before it is being taken away, so if you'll excuse me, good day ladies".

Then she closed the door in the face of the four gossipers, leaving them baffled and offended, on the doorstep.

Ethel was enraged.

"Well I never. The cheek of her, she never even told us her name or what she does. We are none the wiser, that's outrageous. I've never been treated like that in my entire life."

Fuming, Ethel ushered her cronies back down the hill. She was so furious that she marched on without consideration for her three friends struggling to keep up with her.

Behind the closed door, laughing to herself, the weird one made her way to the back of the house. The van driver was standing in the kitchen, next to a box in which laid several beautiful natural arrangements made of wild flowers, plants and twigs.

"Sorry about this Peter. Some busy bodies are intent on finding out who I am and what I do. I know they call me the weird one and they are dying to know more about me. No doubt they are quite disappointed right now."

A hearty laugh came out of her throat and lit up her face.

"Anyway I have worked on the Prince's natural wild flower arrangements so they are ready for you to take with you now. Please thank him once again for giving me a chance to do these and please thank Camilla for her suggestion for the summer arrangements. I will work on them straightaway. See you in a fortnight Peter."

"I'll pass on your message of course. See you then, Laura."

Peter said his goodbyes. He was thinking of the villagers who were so hung up on Laura's appearance that they actually had no idea who was living in their midst…

L
THE LOCKSMITH

Wherever he went, whoever he met, Murgatroy was feared by the villagers.

Murgatroy was a six foot burly man with short, dark, curly hair, a neck as thick as a bull's, and a ruddy complexion (acquired after years spent exposed to intense heat on a daily basis). Despite being an impressive figure of a man, the fear was not caused by his appearance. Nor was it caused by his well-worn leather apron, his big boots, his wide-brimmed hat and a heavy and noisy bunch of keys.

What scared the villagers was the role Murgatroy held in the village of Ash, in Devon. For Murgatroy was a locksmith, but no ordinary locksmith. He was in charge of locking villagers convicted of misdemeanours in the stocks which held pride of place in the centre of the village square. The big, sturdy stocks, built by his grand-father many years before. His own father too had fulfilled the role which Murgatroy had held these last ten years. It was an occupation he greatly enjoyed in addition to his job as a blacksmith, even though it brought mixed feelings. Quite often he relished the power it gave him over the villagers. But it was lonely as no-one was inclined to befriend him. In a way that was the downside of the job. If he had friends, he may be called upon to lock them into the stocks one day if they misbehaved.

In all honesty it didn't take much in 1604 to be punished and locked in the stocks. All it required was a villager to hear somebody swear, then denounce him or her, and the poor bugger ended up into the stocks. Likewise for those who indulged in too much drinking. They soon sobered up after spending hours in stocks snuggly fitting around their ankles, their bare feet exposed, sitting on the ground in all weathers.

The villagers' favourite occupation was to alert each other when one poor miscreant had got himself locked in. They flocked to the square with rotten food, animal excrements or anything else they felt like pelting at the offender.

Being sort of a traditional folk, Murgatroy rarely felt sorry for the villagers he had to lock into the stocks. Firstly, he considered it his duty, and secondly, if they had behaved themselves, his peers would not be in such a predicament. He showed little empathy or compassion to his fellow men who drunk a bit too much or had not curbed their tongues. Some villagers judged him rigid in this thinking.

A man in his early thirties, Murgatroy led what he thought of as an exemplary life, albeit a lonely one at times. Secretly he hankered for a woman to share his life and have children with. There were no woman folks in the village he felt were able to fulfil the role of the locksmith's spouse and mother of his children. So he just went about his business, ignoring the call of the flesh by concentrating on his work and on his highly valued duties as a locksmith.

In the year 1605, on the summer solstice day, a caravan of travellers entered the village of Ash. Throughout the country, this particular June day was dedicated to celebrations. It was not unusual to see travellers passing through the main road on their way to other villages further afield. The caravan was formed of three carriages. The travellers stopped by the fountain on the village square to quench their thirst after several hours of travelling. One of the carriages was causing concern to the driver who made his way to the forge where Murgatroy was working.

The man introduced himself and his fellow travellers as cunning people. In his capacity of locksmith for the village stocks, Murgatroy was an official of the County of Devon and had therefore been informed that cunning people were not to be persecuted. He was aware they were professional practitioners of magic who scoured the whole country. They used their magical charms and spells to combat witchcraft, to locate criminals, to find missing persons and valuable missing property, to influence people to fall in love and more frequently to heal people. Thus they were considered useful unlike the witches who were being hunted and killed as soon as one was identified.

Despite this information, Murgatroy still regarded cunning people with suspicion. He was not a follower of the spiritual craze which had spread like wild fire through the entire country since the mid-1500s. He had witnessed a few disturbing practices in the last few decades which made him weary of anyone claiming to have the ability to heal the sick. He laughed openly at the preposterous allegation that they get people to fall in love through their potions and charms. In reality, Murgatroy was deeply afraid of the curses he had heard they were capable of casting on unsuspecting souls. He feared them like he feared Satan, the devil the church had brainwashed him to fear since he was a child attending mass every Sunday.

The driver explained what he suspected was wrong with the carriage and both he and Murgatroy went outside to inspect it. There were three men around the carriages and maybe nine women, possibly more if some had gone walking around the village. Having identified the problem straight away, Murgatroy took the big wooden wheel off the carriage, rolled it inside the forge and proceeded to fix the damaged cogs. Once the work was completed, the driver asked him if, instead of coins, payment with a flask of a potion selected by Murgatroy was acceptable. The locksmith was taken aback and only just caught himself from cursing. He had nearly uttered a profanity at the suggestion made by the cunning man. What an embarrassment to suffer if he ended up in the stocks himself for swearing.

Thoughts were racing in his head, unsure what to answer the man. As he was pondering whether to accept the proposal or not, a few women he had not noticed earlier, returned to the carriages. One in particular caught his eye. A petite, buxom woman with magnificent long wavy red hair. He estimated that she was about five foot three. From the way she talked with great animation to her companions, he formed the impression that she had a fiery temperament. He didn't know what the conversation was about but, suddenly, he wanted to talk to this woman and get to know her.

A little light came to his mind. To get this woman to fall in love with him, he intended to ask the cunning man for a flask of the love potion. He didn't need any potion himself. One look at her and he was smitten already. His concern was whether she might like him, let alone entertain marrying him. He caught himself by surprise at the thought of marriage. He had not spoken to her and, there he was, imagining her as his wife. Had he gone crazy all of a sudden? Had the driver cast a spell on him? He panicked at this thought. What if this was all a dream he would wake up from without meeting the woman? Worst still, she may not be real.

Murgatroy had to shake himself out of this panic state. This rush of feelings was alien to him. He was unsettled. Nevertheless he turned towards the driver and answered the waiting man:

"Hum, okay, on this occasion I'll accept a potion in return for my services. Tell me, can I use it on someone else?"

"It depends on which potion and who you have in mind?"

The cunning man had followed Murgatroy's gaze to the women outside. He easily read the thoughts tumbling in the big man's mind. It amused him. He had seen this so many times. He saw that Murgatroy was interested in Valia, the red hair healer who had joined the group a couple of years ago after she became a widow. He knew Valia was young enough to want to marry again. But marrying this man and living the rest of her life in this village, may not be what she wished for at this stage. Plus he was so much taller and bigger than she was. However he knew better than to stand in the way of someone's destiny. He already knew Valia and Murgatroy were indeed destined to be together. The damaged wheel was no coincidence. It was all about serendipity.

"Here is the potion you are thinking of. Yes, I know what you have in mind. Her name is Valia and she is ready for marriage again. Slip some of this liquid in her cup when you can and see if she will become agreeable to your advances. Give it a go, blacksmith, and see what happens."

As luck would have it, (or serendipity?) the villagers were celebrating the solstice and invited the stranded travellers to join the feast of food and drinks laid on for the evening. Murgatroy had a place at the top table, him being an official of the County of Devon. These celebrations were always a busy time for Murgatroy though as some folks got so drunk that he would have to put them in the stocks that same night. He hoped he would not be on duty all night as he had his sight set on Valia and getting to know her.

The driver had introduced Murgatroy to his group, including Valia, and they were now sitting at the top table as guests of the village. Valia found herself next to Murgatroy who was preening himself like a peacock. He had managed to slip some of the potion in Valia's cup at the start of the evening. He was happy to see her obvious interest in him. They talked about her life and his work and he became more and more smitten. She was spirited alright and the type of woman he had been waiting for. He was feeling mellow and started enjoying the wine a little too much. Murgatroy had never been a drinker. Tonight, the smell and presence of the woman with the red hair, the love he felt inside, together with the wine he had drunk, all went to his head. He suddenly toppled over blind drunk on the ground.

On hearing the loud thump caused by the fall of this burly man, a big hush failed on the feast. At first, the villagers were stunned to see Murgatroy laying on the ground so drunk. Then they laughed and those who were brave enough approached the man lying on the floor and prodded him to see if he was moving. The women were all giggling.

Poor Murgatroy. Just as well he had passed out, otherwise he would have been mortified by the laughter his fall generated. He had always been such a pillar of respectability. Valia was giggling with the rest of them, but her big heart filled with compassion for this man whom she knew would be her husband soon. This journey to celebrate the solstice had held a different feel for her. She had known deep down that her life would change as a result of it.

She watched as about eight villagers, still sober, carried Murgatroy to the stocks and placed his ankles in it, laying his big body on the bare ground. One of the men had opened it with the key held at Murgatroy's waist. It was sweet revenge for those villagers who had been humiliated on several occasions by the locksmith who had never shown them any mercy for the slightest infringement.

Feeling the early morning sun on his face, Murgatroy suddenly came to. His body was hurting and he realised he was lying on the floor. He tried to move his aching legs but his ankles were encased in the stocks. His head was whirling with embarrassment at the fuzzy recollection of the previous night. Huge shame overcame him. Why had he drank too much? Him, the locksmith for the County of Devon, was finding himself in the stocks? What a disgrace. Then the image of Valia fluttered in front of his eyes. He was dreaming of her, he thought. What would she think of him, drunk and disgraced? Another bout of shame submerged him.

"So, husband to be, how are you feeling today? Sore head, have you?"

Valia was standing in front of him. It had not been a figment of his imagination, she was here, in the flesh looking benevolently down at him, a barely concealed smile on her face.

"I can see you are human after all, blacksmith.

Let's get you out of these stocks. I forced the villagers to give me the key and stopped them from pelting you during the night. You're lucky I was here to take care of you", she declared with enthusiasm.

Despite the intense shame, Murgatroy was elated to see she was not put off by him. And what had she called him earlier? Had she really said "husband to be"? He didn't believe his ears. Life was suddenly looking good. In his mind's eye, he saw a couple of children with bright red hair just like their mother.

The pair walked away from the stocks and Murgatroy never saw the little flask of potion that Valia threw discreetly in a ditch. She was a cunning woman in more ways than one and she knew her potions so well. She had used the perfect one on this big man to bring him to his knees and to a more humane level. She looked forward to her life with the locksmith and to the children she would bear him.

M
MICAELA (POEM FOR MY DAUGHTER)

To be a mother was my dearest wish.
My life was good but something was amiss.
Of my desire to be called Mummy,
For no reason, nature had cheated me.

My body and mind went through hell,
But still, for years, to no avail.
The yearning for a child was so great
That my life became all so grey.

Would I ever know this deep love
That women are born to explore?
This pain was eating at my core,
Of my life I expected so much more.

In my destiny I should have trust
For a child to me it would entrust.

A miracle behind the scene was unfolding,
What a marvellous, unexpected happening.

For there, in the world, searching
Was a child looking for the missing link.
To a young mother she had been born
But in life, she was now on her own.

The first time I saw my daughter
I knew life would be full of laughter.
Bad memories in time will fade
But that special day for life will remain.

Blue-eyed, beautiful cutie
Who sometimes can be so naughty.
She is loving, caring, wild
But above all, Micaela is my child!!!

July 2000

N
NOBODY IS AROUND

It is Sunday again. Every week there is a dreaded Sunday.

Why sun day? I wonder. *What if there is no sun? What if the day is gloomy as it often* is?

To my mind it ought to be called dreaded-day, especially for lonely people with no family around them.

Sunday is supposed to mean love and happiness. For many though, Sundays are far from happy. For those without loved ones to share the day with, Sundays are ghost days. For them, nobody is around.

I am one of these people and it is Sunday. Out of the window I look at passers-by. Many of them are rushing to go to a relative's house for Sunday lunch. Looking at their happy, excited faces, I ask myself;

"Do these people know how lucky they are? Most probably not."

I don't know what they really think of course but I assume they are not aware of their luck. The reason for thinking that way is that I often hear moans from friends with relatives close-by. I also eavesdrop on snippets of conversation in supermarket queues. I witness family dynamics in television programs.

There is always something or someone to moan about: Uncle Jim getting pissed again, Cousin Pat proffering obscenities, Mum being overtired with all the cooking and running around, the annoying sister who cannot stop herself from criticising everybody...

I ponder whether they might appreciate their family more if they experienced loneliness Sunday after Sunday? I am not sure. Maybe they don't know any better. Just like I failed to appreciate my family when things were good.

As a child, I loved Sundays. But as a teenager in the 70s, I came to resent Sundays. Mainly the numerous Sundays spent visiting relatives in the countryside. These visits involved five people squashed in a small car, a one hour journey each way, and no motorway at that time to shorten the travelling time.

Today, alone, far from my own country, the two hour journey to go and eat a lengthy, lively lunch with siblings, parents, cousins, uncles and aunts, sound like heaven. The sense of belonging to a group of people who share common ancestors becomes invaluable to those who have lost it.

It is past lunchtime now. I cast another glance out of the window. The street is now empty. Nobody is around.

I am sitting alone in the front room like many, many Sundays past and future. Reflecting, feeling sad, and wishing yet again that things had turned out differently. A familiar question looms at the forefront of my mind:

"Why on earth did I leave my native country? How was I to know the consequences of a life-changing, impulsive decision? I was merely twenty."

I had thought myself so grown up and brave to leave family and country behind. Until I had lived it, it was impossible for me to have anticipated the loneliness and isolation I often felt over the last forty years. It would have been impossible then to have an inkling of what lay ahead. It was romantic to come to England to be with a man I had fallen in love with and who became my husband.

Had I been warned about what awaited me or told to think twice about leaving my country, I may still have made the same decision. In truth, thousands of people leave their countries of origin for various reasons, but the outcome is frequently the same. More often than not, they come alone, whilst cherished, beloved family members stay behind.

Many, like me, experience the deep loss of having nobody around who cares about them.

In my sixties now, I yearn for a normal family life. The life I had experienced when I was married and my in-laws had become my surrogate family in this land which was not mine. Sadly, the end of the marriage led to the end of family life as I knew it. I had lost my birth family at twenty. I lost the surrogate one twenty years later.

A pervasive feeling of isolation took hold of my heart. It led me to regret being so far from home. I had wanted a life of security, surrounded by loved ones, having a sense of belonging, enjoying family life. That life is long gone and I might never experience it again.

Looking back, did I appreciate my surrogate family enough to see me through the endless, lonely Sundays or other events I would face alone over the years? Those that, at the time, I was unaware would come hurtling at me relentlessly? Christmas, Easter, birthdays, Sundays, important gatherings that families take for granted. With hindsight, most probably not. I missed them even more acutely when I discovered what Sundays felt like for people on their own. The yearning for company, the lack of life around, and the isolation. I didn't bank on the friends being busy with their own loved ones, which you are not part of because it's the weekend.

Ironically, a few years later, I discovered that despite living with someone, Sundays were even lonelier than when alone. A typical case of alone together.

I recall how for years I had loved Sundays when my daughter was at home. They were fun, happy, cherished days. But of course, children grow up and fly the nest. Then Sundays became once more dreaded days.

So, dear members of families around the world, please appreciate your family gatherings. Value the sense of belonging it gives you even though you may not be aware of it.

And, when you are rushing to join your family for Sunday lunch, if you see a solitary figure looking out of the window, spare them a thought. Smile, acknowledge them, wave and make their day. At least, on that particular Sunday, somebody stopped and noticed them. In that brief instant, someone is around for them, making them feel they matter.

0

THE OPENING

I looked at the opening I had created a few moments ago. It had caused me pain and sadness but it had also taken determination simply to carry out my decision. There was no going back. I felt there was no other option. Truly I was not sure how it got that far in the first place. I was only in my twenties, where had it all gone wrong? When had this feeling which permeates my life started weighing on me like a boulder? What had led me to this momentous day?

I thought back to a younger me, at nine years old. Finding out that the hero I worshipped, and had put on a pedestal, had fallen from it with a big bang. My Dad, my hero. Well, how would I know at nine years old what having a nervous breakdown means? What did I know about mental health? It was hard to believe that this man, in my eyes always tall, strong and whom I loved, was the same as this whimpering, crouched up, crying man, rocking in a chair. This man who had fathered three children was now a child himself, requiring more care and attention than his own children.

What were the demons that had brought him to his knees? What had hurt him so badly? I ought to have asked myself these questions but I didn't know. How I regret the ignorance and intolerance of youth which led to judging and finding people lacking. Of course, in my eyes, as my parent, he was infallible and he was supposed to be there for me. That is all I knew then...

Is this the reason for this opening today? Can I really blame it all on him? Was this overwhelming inability to deal with life's ups and downs, a blow to him too? Was the deep wound in his soul a result of growing up without a mother? Or because his father had abandoned him along the way when he married a woman the same age as his own son? What is the point of speculating? He had his own reasons and I may never know them.

Right now I can't fully understand why I am where I am. I am feeling cold. I need to take my mind off the pain. Not the physical pain, that was short-lived. But off the pain at the core of me, the pain in my soul which led me here today. I have a while longer so I dig deep in the recess of my troubled mind to find happy memories to carry with me. Why am I looking for happy moments at this particular time? Maybe it's because I still can't quite believe that the time has come. Everyone around me said my future is ahead of me. That's true. Only their idea of my future is different than my own. However strange as it sounds, I am looking forward to the one I planned for myself. Today, here, this opening is the first step. Yes, I am a bit sad and puzzled but I know what awaits me and I am pleased. My father already knows where I am going. He is expecting me there.

Right now I remember happier times, dancing with him at home when I was younger. Learning the tango and the waltz to music we both loved so much. I owe being a fine dancer to him. He loved dancing. I have carried that same love with me all my life. I am not sure how, but I am back in his arms, dancing my favourite waltz with him. I can hear the music in my head and feel love in my heart. I start humming. I feel warmer and lighter. I know this is the right moment.

I take the knife resting by my side and look at the cut on my left wrist, seeing the life force already seeping out of it slowly, the blood a vibrant red. Then I make a deeper opening on the right wrist. I know I will be with my father soon and the world will feel light and loving.

P

THE PAINTING

Do people ever really know the impact of their words on others? Do they actually comprehend the depth of joy, or sorrow, words can bring? This is a question I have been asking myself from an early age.

It started with the whispers from adults around me, talking to my parents, or behind my parents' back whilst towering above me as a young child. I was not the best looking child amongst my siblings or in our neighbourhood. I often heard comments like "My goodness, she is not pretty, is she?" "Poor child, she is no oil painting, bless her". They said it with a mixture of disdain, superiority, pity and even plain enjoyment at voicing something hurtful to my parents and in turn, later on, hurtful to me. Why would they want to do that to an innocent child?

I guess the reason that people were jealous was that I was born in a powerful family in days gone by.

They relished the fact that we had lost everything. Somehow through their words, they were adding to our shame and disgrace, enjoying a subtle revenge for the lack in their own lives. Still, it was hard to understand their reasons behind such unnecessary nastiness. I had never done anything bad or hurtful to them. I was just being myself. I was loved by my family and that was all I needed. I guess unkindness to some comes more easily than compassion.

As I grew up, I carried on frequently hearing "Hey Liz, you are ugly, by God you are no oil painting. Look at you, ha-ha who will ever want you?" My siblings always protected me from the nastiness of the children. Of course being children they repeated what they had heard their parents say. It did hurt but I was fortunate that, when becoming a teenager, I started to change. After a while the comments stopped bothering me. I was too busy applying myself to learning what I needed to be a good wife, as I knew that soon I would be married. My parents had already promised me to Francesco. Being fourteen years older than me, he seemed so old but I had no say in it. Our families had known each other for a long time so it was obvious I would marry Francesco. I was growing up anyway, my body and my face were changing and I was getting prettier. At least this is what I thought.

So it was, that, when I turned fifteen, I married a

twenty-nine year old man. Yes, in my eyes he was old. However he was wealthy and sort of kind, so my life was not too bad. I had grown into a young woman by then and I knew that he found me pretty. I knew because he told me often. We lived in a lovely house in a beautiful town full of cathedrals, churches and art. Soon our marriage was blessed with children (in fact I ended up having six of them). We had three boys and three girls. I felt sad when we sent my eldest daughter to a convent when she was twelve. I know it was a necessary tradition as providing her with a dowry for a suitable marriage was impossible for us but it broke my heart.

A few years into our married life, through our church, Francesco met a young artist who lived with his father. When our second son Andrea was born, Francesco asked the young man to paint a portrait of me. He wanted to hang the painting in our home. I felt such a mature woman posing for a portrait. I was officially a Dona, a respected married woman, despite my youth.

It was a lengthy process though. It took hours of my time, sitting looking serene, whilst all I felt was sadness inside me, thinking of my poor girl in the convent. It took a good few years of sitting for most of the portrait to be painted. During that time my daughter died in the convent. She was only nineteen and from then on, sadness left its imprint on my face, robbing me of joy, and life in general became a struggle.

Leo was brilliant, he understood my sorrow and knew I didn't have the heart to smile for him anymore. Thinking back, I never envisaged anyone ever wanting to paint me, Lisa Da Gioncodo, let alone being painted by one of the rising artists in Florence.

Little did I know that, centuries later, thanks to Leonardo's skills, my face would end up being one of the most expensive and the most famous oil painting portrait in the entire world.

Wouldn't it be wonderful to have been able to see the faces of the people commenting on my looks all those years ago? Quite honestly this feels to me like Poetic Justice…

Q
THE QUAGMIRE OF HUMAN GREED OR COVID 19
(POEM)

The planet is groaning,
Mother Earth is chastising,
Nature is rebelling,
Human destruction needs stopping!
Creatures of all kinds yearn for freedom;
They cry "Enough of the martyrdom".
Animals in all countries took action
To prevent further their habitat destruction.
On humans they have exacted their revenge
To force the quagmire to change.
On humans the earth struck a major blow
Affecting what they revere; their cash flow.
Humans are asked to stay in for a while,
Most of them complaining "this is vile".
Unwilling to live indoors for weeks as recluse
To abide by the rules many, of course, refuse.
As all species, human or animals, are connected,

For the sake of the planet, Covid 19 must be
deflected.
Meanwhile, nature is breathing out of its every pore.
Many once-hidden sounds unexpectedly come to
the fore
The sky is a dazzling blue, devoid of airplanes, the
air is clean,
The chirpy birds are elated, the grass is a rich vibrant
green.
In the spring of 2020 the world toppled over:
Oxygen became more valuable than silver,
Whilst some greedily got over nourished,
Too many around the world tragically perished.
There is no knowing what the future has in store
But one thing is sure, nothing will be like before.
To further destroy the earth is no longer an option
Nature has rebelled and is seeking retribution.

April 2020

R
A RENDEZ-VOUS TO REMEMBER

Is this man for real? Wow, what a refreshing sight?

Angela felt a stirring in her heart, a glimpse of some brighter future edging slowly into her consciousness. Though she was still unaware of the full impact of this rendez-vous between the man, her husband and herself.

After all these years, he is sitting here, in my living room. Sitting on my settee, my Buddy nestled next to him, lapping every bit of his attention. Wow, he is even stroking the dog's ears.

She recognised the well-honed casual gesture so familiar to dog owners. But of course he would do, as he owned a dog.

Fancy a man sitting next to Buddy and not making a fuss about germs. It does exist then?

There were both sadness and hope in this question. This relaxed scene of man and dog was a big revelation. For Buddy's unexpected arrival in his new home the previous year had caused a divide between her and her husband. Angela had fallen head over heels in love with her dog and considered him a member of the family. The problem arose when her husband saw him as an animal to be kept at a distance and not as a beloved pet like she did.

What was surreal for Angela was that today, was the first time she had met Gregory. She thought back to the last five years when she had heard his name mentioned so many times. She had never spoken to him, or even met him, but she knew of him.

He had been the subject of quite a few discussions when her husband had been doing some work with him. Even after they had gone their separate ways, her husband had maintained contact so she kept hearing about Gregory. She had no idea who the man was behind the name but she was curious about him.

At last I meet him. I feel I have known him for years. He is nothing like I imagined though. I never realised he was so tall, dynamic and chatty. Actually, I like him.

Listening to the men talking, she liked the camaraderie between Gregory and her husband. Gregory was drinking his tea, talking, quite undisturbed by the dog wanting attention from this new visitor. She witnessed his hands going from Buddy to his cup of tea without any fuss made.

At least Gregory doesn't ask to wash his hands every five minutes!

Gregory was clearly someone who was not neurotic about germs when stroking a dog, neither did he display OCD tendencies. This casual behaviour was an unusual occurence for Angela. This acceptance of the dog as a source of joy was what she had hoped for from her husband. Unfortunately it had all turn into a bit of a nightmare.

She saw how different life could be. It shook her so much that, there and then, Angela made a decision that would change her life. She knew her marriage had been over for some time for various reasons. She had held off taking action as she feared that a break-up would lead to an uncertain future. But the divide, stress, sadness and arguments caused by Buddy's arrival were wearing her down and made life less than pleasant.

These arguments have to end. I am so tired of feeling like a leper. It's time to move on. Maybe there is hope for me. Maybe I can one day find my own Gregory. Imagine being with a man who would not pull away because I have just hugged the dog. A man who would not refuse to hold my hand because I have stroked Buddy. Someone who doesn't strip the skin off his hands after washing every time he touches the dog...

This prospect was soothing her broken heart. A little bit of light was filtering at last through the heavy darkness inhabiting her soul for many months. She knew there would be rough times ahead, but Buddy was her faithful companion. He was the one she had chosen to remain in her life.

So if ever there was a rendez-vous to remember, a rendez-vous that changed someone's future, it's the day Angela met Gregory. For the day she saw Gregory and Buddy together, the future opened up and looked decidedly brighter. Out there somewhere in time, she would find her own Gregory. She imagined the two of them sitting on the settee, side by side, with Buddy on their lap.

Who knows, we might even push the boat out and get a second dog!

S
MY SUPERPOWER

Today I woke up in my bed, that same one I have been confined to for years. I woke up but something felt somewhat different this morning. My body was light, no longer this big boulder which had been dragging me down for most of my life. My head and my heart were full of joy and happiness. Feeling both light & airy. Emotions I didn't often feel. Generally I was too busy coping with the day to day challenges of this illness that kept me crippled.

All of a sudden I was unsure what to do. This feeling of lightness was not one I was familiar with. I closed my eyes, blinked a few times, and finally reopened them, hoping, fearing all at once, that the lightness was still here. It was. I had heard that if you wished it hard enough, you were able to acquire superpowers. So for weeks now, I had wished and wished to be able to fly away from this bed, to escape the confines of this stifling room. My wish had been granted. I had been given my superpower. At last today I will fly and see a world I have never known.

I had dreamt I flew over snowy mountains, catching falling snowflakes in my open mouth. I had even felt my lungs deeply fill with the fresh mountain air instead of the stale air of my room. I had seen myself fly over the oceans, observing the motion of the waves, the ripples of the sand under the water, the underwater life. All the sea creatures alive and well, swimming, jumping, making the most of life.

I had dreamt I flew over deserts, feeling the sun and dry heat on my cold skin. Perhaps even spot an oasis to rest under its shade for a moment. I had dreamt I flew over hills and meadows, smelling the wild flowers, touching them with a stroke of my hand as I passed gently over their beautiful, upturned, colourful heads.

I had dreamt I felt the cool wetness of the river, dipping a toe in as I hovered over the running water for a second. I had yearned to see cows, sheep, rabbits and every animal possible in the valley beneath me. Animals I had heard of in my story books but had never seen. I had imagined coming face to face with all types of birds soaring in the sky, pondering on this strange specimen with sticks hanging from its body, but no wings.

What would it be like to really fly? Arms outstretched, legs resting on the blue line of the horizon, the wind supporting my emaciated, useless body. To fly in the white fluffy clouds. To pick at them with greed. Just like I had picked at the candy floss someone brought me a long, long time ago, when I was a mere child.

I was so eager to see it all. This big world I had heard of and had never explored beyond the boundaries of my room. Full of glee and wonderment, I ventured further and further afield, oblivious of any tiredness, my weightless body carried in the air. I only needed to think of a place and, by magic, I was transported there.

Soon, I had seen all the famous places I had dreamt of. So I wished with all my heart to go and meet people like me. People who had been suffering for years and who, today, were flying away from the prison of their bodies. I was flying over a city full of fire, noise, explosions, and screaming. The suffering of the people below was tangible. I vaguely recalled reading about war zones. Had I stumbled across one? It was not what I had wanted to fly to.

Suddenly, I heard a loud explosion, wailing and piercing screams below. Right in front of me, a group of bloodied, small children were flying just like me, their arms outstretched, puzzlement on their faces. We touched hands and held each other as we flew up and up as if we were never going to reach the end of the sky. We were all so light, flying towards a white light. I knew I would never see my dreary room again. At long last my dearest wish had been granted. I had managed to fly out of my body and out of my life. I had escaped.

That day though, the world learnt on the evening news that a group of children had been killed by a massive explosion in Syria and ten children had died in one fell swoop…

T

THERE ARE NO MORE STRAY DOGS IN HOLLAND

It was cold and wet. I was tired. I had been roaming the streets in search of a bite to eat for days now. My body was itchy. Every time, I wanted to scratch my neck, the pain in my back legs and in my whole body was horrible. My neck felt like needles pricking me relentlessly. My paws were sore and flaky and one of my back leg was broken. A big man had kicked me when I had approached him for food. Something the man was carrying smelt so nice, like chicken or something. I came near him, with my tongue hanging out, hoping against all odds for a little scrap. Instead of a bit of food, I felt the pain of a strong sideways kick in my left leg. I yelped loudly as the pain was intense. I learned from this and always kept my distance from humans after that.

Today I am disheartened, I am in pain. I am tired. I am hungry. I am lonely and I have decided to just lie there, on the side of the road. The cars pass by me but I am no longer scared. I don't want to live anymore. Since I was born in the bushes by the side of the road (a few months ago I think), I have learned that humans cannot be trusted. I lost my mummy. She went away to look for food one day but never came back to where she had hidden me. I had my little brother for a while but he too disappeared one day, taken by a group of kids. I hope they were nice to him. The other one, my little sister, was too weak. Sadly when mummy didn't come back, she died. I will always remember her stiff little body next to mine. I thought she was asleep. I licked her like I used to do every day, but she felt cold. She didn't lick me back. I understood I was all alone now.

I hear a noise but it is so hard to lift my head in its direction. I vaguely see some shapes and hear sounds getting closer to me. I don't know what it is and I don't care. But wait. Someone is coming closer to me, hand stretched out near me, holding tempting bits of food. I have to lift my head and find out what it is. I see morsels on the ground. I want them. They smell so nice. But I am wary. Who are you? What are you going to do to me? I find the strength to pull my tongue out to reach for the delicious scraps. I bring them back to my hungry mouth. Others follow which I nab quickly too. At this point I am not even wary anymore. I don't have the strength to be. What is happening? All of a sudden, I feel an unfamiliar touch on my head. I hesitate. Shall I accept the touch or growl? I have no energy to fight so I let the hand gently stroke me. I sniff the hand and feel the gentle energy of this human in front of me. His eyes are kind and his touch feels good. Plus the morsels he gives me are so welcome, I decide to trust him.

"Here, Lars, bring the cage. I found the puppy. He looks in a bad way. Call the vet and tell him we are bringing a dog in shortly."

Whilst talking in a soothing voice, Christian suddenly picked me up and held me against him. "Here, poor little guy, don't worry we got you now. We will take care of you. "

I had no idea that I had been seen by a member of the animal police patrol. Thanks to him, my future looked happier than it did a while ago. You see, I am one of the numerous stray dogs in the Netherlands being rescued, treated, neutered and placed in a rescue centre until I am adopted. Had I been born in another country, I more than likely would have been put to sleep by now. Instead, they fixed me up and found me a forever home.

I can't tell you how much I love my hoomans. Slowly, I learn I can trust again. They love me and play with me. They give me food, not just once, but twice a day. I am growing well, they say. My neck is no longer itchy, my leg is fixed and I can run in the fields just outside a town called Amsterdam. I meet lots of doggy pals on walks. Shall I tell you why? Well, in the beautiful country where I was born, most hoomans have a dog. Plenty of friends to meet and play with. At last, I'm in heaven. Earth heaven. I thank my lucky star every day to be a little Dutch dog!

U

THE UNSWERVING SLUG (POEM)

The slug knows where it has to go
No need for drama, no need for big ego.
Onward it goes, its body stretching,
Inch by inch slithering, unswerving.
No leaf or twig too big, no diversion,
For the slug's life is all about action.
Fascinated, its steady journey I observe
From its goal, nothing makes it swerve.
Slowly does it, up and down blades of grass,
No matter what, the slug follows it compass.
From this small critter what can we learn?
That with focus, what you want, you will earn.
Whatever your size, from your path, don't waver,
With a constant pace, you'll get there sooner or later,
Always reach for what you know you deserve
And let nothing or no one make you swerve…
…This is the slug's philosophy of life…

V
VÉLO SIR APTOR

Sebastian (or Seb as he prefers to be called) is a quiet, four year-old boy. He is an only child so he has to find ways to entertain himself. He often plays alone in his room with different toys or he looks at simple story books. What he likes best though is being outdoors, running around or going on the swing his parents installed in the garden. Sometimes his mum plays with him or friends come around and then it's all hell let loose. They play hide and seek either in the garden or in the house or play "it".

In the summer they play outside with small water pistols or splash in a small pool. Fun and laughter is on the agenda, just as it should be. In short, Seb is a toddler enjoying his childhood. No digital equipment needed, no spending hours in front of the TV, just good old-fashion fun with his fellow toddlers.

Alice, Seb's mum, is French. As his speech is

developing, she teaches him some little words; the names of animals, things, colours, toys and whatever she can think of on a daily basis. He is able to name the picture of items he identifies on little tiles she shows him. In fact, he is quite good at this. Alice knows his accent leaves a lot to be desired, but at four years old it is not an issue.

Of course, growing up, Seb learns to say words in English, his own language, starting like most babies do with daddy and mummy. He gradually builds up his vocabulary and, from one day to the next, becomes the chatter box that toddlers tend to become. Like most parents, Alice was eager for Seb to talk but at times she wishes he would just be quiet for a little bit. Every so often Seb utters new words with gusto and excitement.

One day, his mum shows him pictures of modes of transport. She teaches him the French words: 'voiture', 'train', 'bateau', 'vélo', 'bus' and 'avion'.

Seb is enthusiastic in his learning and keeps repeating: voiture – car, train - train, vélo - bike, avion – plane, autobus - bus, bateau – boat.

They play a little game where Alice mimes a mode of transport and he guesses what it is. He thinks it is such fun. Both mother and son enjoy the game and it helps Seb learn quickly.

Growing up, beyond learning French and playing with his friends, Seb has one passion;

dinosaurs. He plays with plastic ones of all shapes and sizes. He is fond of watching "The Land Before Time", a cartoon full of dinosaurs in prehistoric times. He sits with his face full of wonderment at the characters. There are all different types of dinosaurs and, for the most part, all friends with each other. Seb insists from time to time that his mother sits with him to watch the cartoon. Alice obliges for ten minutes then leaves him to it and gets on with her chores. But she can understand his fascination with the cartoon. Watching it with Seb, she learns quite a lot about dinosaurs too. She sees how animated Seb becomes watching the characters and the story. It is the only one he is interested in despite an extensive collection of other children's DVDs. An idea is taking shape in her mind. A seed has been planted. Now she has to find a way of bringing this to fruition.

Seb's fifth birthday is approaching. His parents are wondering what to buy him. His dad thinks a bike is an ideal present especially as he is a keen cyclist himself. The thought of cycling with his little boy at some point is an attractive prospect. A good way to develop a father and son bond, creating special moments which will stay with a child forever. He mentions it to Alice.

"Brilliant present. Who better than you to teach him how to ride a bike? Then I too will ride my bike with him to go to the park. Oh Danny, quelle bonne idée!"

"Okay. I'll ask my mum to have Seb for a couple of hours this weekend and we'll go and buy one."

Alice realises that with this present she has a chance to carry out her unusual idea. She keeps what she has in mind a secret from both Seb and Danny. When they get to the shop, Alice is adamant that she wants a green bike.

"Really. I like the shiny blue one here and I think Seb will like it too".

"Yes, I know Seb will like it but I think the green is more original, more him. Blue is always associated with boys, so let's go for green. Just to be different. This bike here is perfect. Come on let's ask the sales assistant."

Alice bluffs to convince Danny to buy the green one. Seeing how insistent Alice is, he agrees.

"Well I guess you have a point. Anyway as long as Seb has a bike, he'll be happy whatever the colour. "

The green bike is brought home and finds its way to the loft, hidden until the following Saturday when Seb turns five.

On the Monday, Alice gathers all the newspapers in the house then goes to buy some essential items for her exciting project. She works tirelessly, in the loft, whilst Seb is at school. Danny has no idea what is going on. Alice is pleased with how creative she is and how her project is progressing.

After four days, it is finished. Alice admires her handy work and cannot help but chuckle to herself, thinking of Seb's face when he sees his bike. The present is ready.

The long awaited birthday arrives. The child is so excited that he wakes his parents early.

"Mummy, Daddy it's my birthday, wake up, wake up Mummy. Where is my present? Come on, wake up, Daddy".

He jumps on the bed and shakes them both to make sure they wake up and pay attention to him.

Although shaken roughly by their boy, Danny and Alice pretend to sleep a bit longer.

"Mummy, come on I want my pressie."

Amused, Alice opens her eyes. Seb's face is staring at her. She sees such excitement and anticipation in his eyes and on his lovely face, that she elbows Danny to get up and get a move on. She doesn't have the heart to make Seb wait any longer. Besides she too is excited to see his reaction to his present.

"Happy Birthday Seb. Now close your eyes. No peeping. Daddy will guide you to your present. You're coming Danny?

"Of course I am. Come here champ."

Danny scoops his little boy in his arms in a half

affectionate, half playful tackle. He tickles Seb's tummy then shields the boy's eyes with one of his hands. Both father and son are giggling.

"Close your eyes now like mummy said and let's go see your present."

Alice has gone on ahead to the front room. She had reassured Danny last night that she would bring the bike down from the loft, ready for this morning. She is standing in front of the present. The back of a child's bike sticks out but the front is hidden by her body.

"Daddy, is the bike for me? Cool."

"Yes, it's yours champ. Hang on, what's this Alice?"

Danny is pointing at the strangely coloured bits sticking out at the front of the bike, not completely concealed by Alice's body.

"It looks like an animal."

Both man and boy are baffled. Danny knows they bought a bike but this does not look like the one they chose together. Alice steps aside to reveal the present. She grins and pride is written all over her face. Gasps come out of both father and son's mouths.

"Oh wow, mummy what is it, what is it? Tell me."

"This Seb, is your very own Vélo Sir Aptor.... Your dinosaur bike." She is laughing at the name which she came up with a while back. It makes her laugh every time she thinks about it.

At first the child is a bit stunned. Not quite taking it all in or understanding what he is seeing. All of a sudden, Seb claps his hands and rushes towards the velociraptor's head adorning the handle bar of his new bike. He looks at the head closely and hugs it carefully.

"Mummy, it looks like little a proper dinosaur. I love it mummy. Thank you."

Danny claps too.

"Golly! Alice this is amazing. I have never, ever seen a bike look like a dinosaur. It looks so good. Let me take a picture and we can whatsapp it to everybody. You're such a clever woman. Isn't she a clever mummy Seb? I love your bike."

Seb is happy and fascinated. He is inspecting the head of the velociraptor made of papier maché that his mother had modelled on the little dinosaur in his favourite DVD. He knows he has the best bike and that his friends will never have one the same. He loves dinosaurs, he loves bikes and now he has both on his very own cool vélo.

"Bravo Alice!"

W

WHAT DO YOU WANT FROM ME?

"Oh no. There it goes again…"

This repetitive *"what do you want from me?"* I hear through the thin walls of my flat… Since moving in 6 months ago, I keep hearing the woman next door ask *"what do you want from me?"* on a regular basis. Although it is muffled, she sounds quite distressed at times. What is going on in that flat? Is she having an argument with her husband? I am baffled because when I see the young couple in the street, they seem happy and loving so what is causing their recurring argument indoors and her distress?

I do not want to be nosy but my mind is going round and round imagining all kinds of possibilities.

"Is he trying to get money from her? Is he unhappy with the way she keeps the flat?" Maybe my imagination is getting the better of me because I start extrapolating:

"What does her husband want her to do? Is he putting strange demands on her she is not happy with? Do they have a secret room next to mine?"

It occurred to me I may have read "Fifty shades of grey" too many times in the last year.

Perhaps I should go and introduce myself and see what information I can gather. But then again, she is unlikely to say *what do you want from me?* in my presence. She seems well mannered so I suspect that there would be no argument in front of the next door neighbour. It surprises me a bit though that I never seem to hear his answers or whatever he said to prompt the now familiar outburst *what do you want from me?*

Still this is driving me crazy. I need to get to the bottom of this distressing and unusual situation. I need to find out what is going one way or another. I decide that next time I see the couple in the street, I will go up to them, strike up a conversation and see what I can glean through subtle questioning. I am beginning to feel like a detective trying to crack a case and I am partly apprehensive, partly excited to finally get a chance to discover their "secret".

Happy with this new strategy in mind I was going to act on it when I suddenly realise that there is an eerie silence next door.

Come to think of it, I had not heard any outburst

since the day before yesterday. Well this is something. Pheww! Peace at last.

But of course I start to worry. Has anything happened to her? Has he harmed her in some way? Has the argument taken untold proportions? My head is spinning with even more elaborate possibilities than before. I am so confused and stressed about it that I have to get some fresh air.

I walk to the high street and guess who I see. Her. From next door. What a relief, she is alive... She is coming out of the local corner shop, head down, crying. My god, perhaps something serious has happened after all, something bad enough to make her cry in the street? I stop and introduce myself.

She looks up, upset so I ask her "Are you ok?"

Her throat heavy with sobs she answers "No, not really, our beloved parrot died a couple of days ago."

"I am so sorry", I didn't realise you had a parrot".

"Oh really", said my neighbour, "you must have heard it... his favourite sentence was *what do you want from me?*"...

X
A XMAS TALE

Winter 2017, my first ever winter. Winter is great because Xmas is in winter. I was only four months old so imagine the excitement I felt with Xmas and then the snow. I loved my first winter.

Wow! What a magical time that was. First, I went to my sister and her boyfriend. Mummy drove us there of course. When we arrived, I was so eager to see her, to get a cuddle from her and to get into her lovely house. But when she carried me in, I realised the front room looked different.

My sis had put up, inside the room, a big green tree with branches that are a bit prickly. That was a bit strange for me but she told me it was a big Xmas tree. It was beautifully decorated with shiny tinsels and bright coloured round balls. It looked amazing, tantalising, exciting and tempting all at once. I was gazing at all of it. My eyes caught the reflection of the lights on the balls and onto the walls. I was feeling this urge inside to follow all the rays of light going around the room. It formed pretty patterns and I had never seen anything as shiny as this before. But then again what did I know at four months old?

There were boxes and bags under the tree. All different shapes, with colourful paper too, in lovely colours. Sis held up two of them for me to see. She said they were for me so I was eager to open them, but of course I was not able to do so by myself. I had to be patient and wait for mummy to help me on Xmas morning. I was not sure what was in mine. The excitement of wanting to know and trying to guess was making me feel giddy and silly all at once. In the end I was so excited that I fell asleep. After my rest, I had forgotten all about the presents.

Instead I became aware that the smell at my sis' house was out of this world. I didn't know where or what to smell next. There were so many smells coming out of the kitchen throughout the whole house. My nose was assaulted every which way by smells of meat cooking, of fish frying and of cakes baking. So much to smell and only one little nose to smell them with. What a Xmas eve.

Finally on Xmas day, before lunch sis, her boyfriend Jaco and mummy wore silly hats in red and green. They called them Xmas hats and mum even said "we look like elves."

Not sure what it was we were looking like but she seemed happy about being an "elves", so I was happy too. Then sis took lots of "selfies" of the four of us. Then hey presto, we magically had a smiling Xmas picture to send to everyone we love on that Xmas day. When they received the picture, people all said how cute we all looked, especially me, being so little.

The only sad thing was that Dad was not in the picture. He was at home working. He works a lot, and that Xmas I missed his smiles and his tickles. I like spending time with him but he is always busy.

Anyway, I am losing track of my thoughts. (Mummy says this all the time.)

Then I saw the white stuff drop from the sky on Boxing Day. Why is it called Boxing Day anyway? I didn't see anyone boxing that day or even any boxes anywhere... All the presents had already been opened so no more enticing secrets under the tree to uncover. But I am getting lost in my thoughts again.

That Boxing day morning, Mummy left to go back home without me. I was spending a few days with my sis. That was a real treat; I had her all to myself and I felt all grown up. I love my sis, she is the best. She takes good care of me. She makes sure I am warm, fed and loved.

That morning after Mummy left, we were out together when white stuff was falling from the sky.

My eyes struggled to follow all the tiny little bits of fluffy stuff floating around us. They looked like water drops in the shower when mummy gives me a bath. I looked down and saw a white carpet on the ground, on the trees and on the roofs of houses. I was pretty sure it was not there the night before or when I had visited her house before. I didn't know what to make of it. I was well wrapped up but my feet still felt a bit cold. I got all silly of course. I wanted to catch these fluffy things on my tongue and with my nose, so I went all giddy again…

That was such fun, I was happy, sis was happy. Winter is truly magical, so many lovely things happened to me on my first winter. A loving family, a warm home, lovely food, Xmas presents, fun and laughter and lots of play.

By the way, I forgot to tell you; my name is Teddy. Last winter I was a small puppy so excited about his first winter that I didn't stop wagging my winter's tail. And this young dog is now looking forward to Xmas again this year, especially as Dad will be there with us. He makes my Xmas tail, winter's tail, summer's tail and any time's tail wag so much when he tickles me….

Y
YOU TOLD ME YOU WOULDN'T DO THAT

To think I believed you. You told me you wouldn't do that. But that was rubbish and you know it. Stupidly, I fell for it, hook, line and sinker.

Of course I know now that you never really meant it. All the years you took me (and her) for a ride. The years you took me for granted, whilst getting involved more deeply with her. You and her, out together behind my back. Many times. And you thought I didn't know.

When I set eyes on her for the very first time, I knew there would be trouble. She looked so innocent that, there and then, I just knew she would steal you from me at some point and cause trouble. Indeed, the bitch has been pulling at your heart for nine years now.

But to actually do that? To even consider doing it in the first place? What made you think it would be acceptable? Was it all your idea or hers? You are a professional man, did you imagine this was acceptable? That this craziness was appropriate? Did you, at any point, stop and think of the repercussions on your work and on our relationship? How will your clients react to this? Would it portray you as a serious, reliable and trustworthy man?

You had briefly discussed your plan with me. You saw dismay and unhappiness on my face. I firmly said no, and brought your attention to the flaws in your plan. But it didn't stop you from going ahead, did it? How could you? After you told me that you wouldn't do that? Well, I was right, she has finally won, she is with you forever and I am unhappy about it.

When did you start thinking about her being permanently so close to your heart? Why her and not me? I am your wife, your right hand person, after all. It is unsettling to have to see her face every time I look at your body. I know you love Molly to bits and enjoy taking her for a ride in the car and walk with her. But who has ever heard of a forty five year old man sporting the tattoo of a scruffy dog's head on his chest?

Z

ZAYLA AND THE SECRET

Ushering Adelson towards the school hut for his first day at secondary school, his mother Zayla is transported back to a similar day years ago, the day she met the new teacher at the secondary school. She was 11 years old.

She is a child again setting off to school like Adelson. She is with her best friend Dodi. The girls have to walk for one hour to reach the school.

That morning at the start of their walk, Dodi turns to Zayla with an enigmatic smirk.

"I have a secret."

Dodi comes near Zayla, cups her hand around her friend's ear and whispers her secret. She doesn't dare speak it out loud. It might make it real.

The secret Zayla hears is not unusual in her native Africa. Still it scares her. Zayla pulls away from her friend in shock.

"Where did you hear that Dodi? You don't even know it's true."

She too is scared that saying the words would bring the secret to life.

"I heard it from Sany. The preacher told her parents. So there."

"I can't believe it. What are we gonna do, Dodi? I like going to school but now I am scared to go. I don't want no new teacher with a horrid secret. "

Zayla is shaking and her eyes starts to fill up. She looks pathetic and scared and Dodi laughs at her.

"Stop being a cry baby Zayla, what can she do to us? She isn't gonna do anything weird to us in the school. Let's run to meet this Miss Tomei or we'll be late. Then something bad will really happen."

Dodi laughs, sounding like a hyena. Zayla feels even less eager to go to school and meet Miss Tomei.

"Hey, Dodi. Wait for me."

Dodi is sprinting ahead. Zayla runs on the dusty road to catch her up. The sun is already quite warm.

Dodi points out to something in the distance. Zayla follows the direction of her finger.

"Look, a dead goat. It looks like it's been here a few days. Come on lets kick the bones, it will be fun."

Both girls are keen to break the boredom of the walk and run to the dead mass. One part of the journey is through the savannah so sometimes there are carcasses of dead animals, killed by a wild predator. Lots of bones to kick mean lots of fun.

Parts of the journey are scary for the children going to the school but they have no choice. Zayla and Dodi's dads told them which way to walk to avoid coming face to face with lions or a leopard. In Africa, going to school is the only way to have a good future and a good life. Maybe not as good as the life of children in Europe, but much better than some of the older Africans who didn't have the chance to go to school. So even if the walk is long and there is a risk to be chased by wild animals, that is what has to be done to get an education.

Zayla has been worrying about the secret since the two friends set off for school.

"Maybe I should tell Mae and Pai? I guess I should but what if they stop me going to school? I want to be a teacher one day so I want to learn. I love learning."

"Zayla you are so stupid. You tell your parents and you can be sure no-one will be allowed to go to school. That's what you want? Let's work out a plan to find out if she is one of them or not. But we have to be careful. We don't want any bad thing to happen to us."

"Yes you're right we need to know. When we arrive at school, shall I pretend to be ill? And see what she says or what she does?"

"Good idea, Zayla. Hurry up, now. It's getting late."

Relieved to have a plan the girls run the rest of the way.

When they finally arrive Miss Tomei is standing outside the hut used as a school. She is waiting for all the children to go in and settle. She is a tall, young woman. She has some scars across both cheeks, sort of like criss-cross welts. They are raised and white, quite striking against her black skin. When she goes inside the hut, the children notice she is limping on her right leg. Miss Tomei looks different to what Zayla expected.

Wow, I think she's cool. Look at those scars on her face. And her leg. What happened to her leg? Who did that to her face?

Zayla doesn't voice her admiration of Miss Tomei aloud for fear of being ridiculed by her so called friend. Dodi would not understand that Miss Tomei's scars, limp and also her teaching ability, give her kudos in Zayla's eyes.

The girls are the last to find a seat in the hut and they hear Miss Tomei address the children.

"Settle down now. I need to talk to you all, so be quiet please."

The children hold their breath and some elbow each other in the ribs. Dodi winks to Zayla and nods her head as if to say "let's see what she is gonna say."

Before the teacher had a chance to speak, Dodi calls out.

"Good morning Miss. I'm Dodi and this is Zayla, She isn't feeling well today, her tummy hurts she said. Can you help her? "

"Hello Dodi. Hello Zayla. Don't worry. Come with me Zayla. I know how to make you better."

Oh no, what is she going to do? I should have kept my mouth shut. Silly Dodi, putting this funny idea in my head. What do I do now?

Before Zayla can answer her own question she is pulled by the hand by Miss Tomei who directs her towards a table on the far side of the hut. On it are various books, papers, pens and a few small bottles filled with liquid of various colours. Miss Tomei takes one with a bright red liquid inside and hands it to Zayla to drink. It looks like a bottle of blood.

"Don't worry child, I know this potion will ease your stomach pain. Come on, drink up."

Remembering the secret Dodi told her, Zayla is scared. She is unsure what to do. She starts shaking. The bottle she was holding falls on the mud floor. Suddenly she sees Miss Tomei's eyes turn red. Red like the devil's eyes. Behind her a strange laugh is echoing around the hut.

At this moment Zayla has no doubt that Miss Tomei is the mad witch the preacher accuses her of being. She pushes past Miss Tomei and runs out of the hut. She hears the hyena laugh erupting from Dodi again.

She does not stop to ask Dodi why she is laughing. She runs a short distance until she stumbles and falls on the rough dusty ground. Hurt and scared, she hears a voice behind her.

"Zayla, are you hurt? Can you get up?"

Oh no it's Miss Tomei. What she gonna do to me now? She must be angry with me.

"Zayla, listen to me. I know what is happening. I was going to talk to all of you about something before your friend Dodi interrupted me. I was about to say that a nasty preacher has been going around spreading rumours that I am a witch. I wanted to warn you all not to pay attention to it. But you and Dodi heard the rumour already eh?"

"Yes, Dodi told me this morning. I was scared. I want to come to school but I don't want a teacher who is a witch. Then Dodi said to try to catch you out by saying I was ill. I'm sorry."

"It was not your fault Zayla. The preacher bears a grudge against my family and wants to discredit me. But your friend Dodi should not spread rumours without knowing the truth of it. Let that be a lesson to both of you. Gossips can be dangerous. Especially in Africa where witchcraft scares folks so much. Let's return to the hut and start our lesson."

Relieved Zayla gets up and walks back with Miss

Tomei. The accusation that she was a witch had weighed heavily on Zayla's mind. Then when Miss Tomei gave her the potion, she had seen what she wanted to see.

Phew, I am glad she explained it all. Stupid Dodi causing all this hassle and worry. That's bad. Gossip is bad.

She thinks she hears her teacher mutter something as they enter the hut. Dodi is waiting for them. Laughing. Suddenly she clenches her stomach and rushes outside to be sick. Pupils concentrating on Dodi do not notice the contented smile on Miss Tomei's face. Neither had they noticed the signs she did with her fingers when she had gone past Dodi seconds ago.

"A witch, me? As if."

POSTSCRIPT

Dear Reader,

Thank you for choosing my book.

If you enjoyed these unusual stories, please feel free to leave a comment on my Facebook page: Andrée Roby@RegineDem. Your feedback is welcome.

My first book "Double Vision", a creative crime drama, is available on Amazon.

Until the next book, all the best.

Andrée x

After spending over 35 years in South London, Andrée Roby, originally from France, now lives in West Sussex.

As a language teacher, she loves languages and the written word. She has published flash fiction, poems and articles, some of which are featured in the "A to Z of original poems, flash fiction and short stories". In this mixed genre collection, the author shows her versatility and imagination as each story relates to a letter of the alphabet.

In addition, Andrée Roby was inspired by masters of thriller/crime novels to write her own murder story and her first novella "Double Vision" was published in January 2019. It was voted Book of the Month UK for April 2019 by the publisher Tredition.

She is currently working on her second book "Failed Vision" and on the translation of "Double Vision" into French.

Printed in Great Britain
by Amazon